MOSTLY TRUE II:
EPISODES

Arlene N. Cohen

Mostly True II: Episodes

ISBN: 978-0-578-72948-0

A catalog record for this book is available from the Library of Congress

Edited by Sarah Beach

Dedication

*To Roshis Robert and Anne Aitken who taught me how to meditate
and take one step at a time and to Betty Jones and Marcus Bugler, my
beloved dance teachers, who taught me how to fall up and spin.*

Other Books by Arlene

Stories on the Move: Integrating Literature and
Movement with Children from Infant to Age 14 (2007)
Published by Libraries Unlimited/ABC-CLIO

Mostly True: Short Stories, 2020

Literacy on the Move Series: (2020)
The Dancing Chameleons (for ages 2-6)
The Dancing Reptiles (for ages 4-8)
The Dancing Dogs (for ages 6-10)
The Dancing Chameleons Coloring and Activity Book
The Dancing Reptiles Coloring and Activity Book
The Dancing Dogs Coloring and Activity Book

Contents

Introduction:

In my first book in this series, ***Mostly True: Short Stories***, we traveled on the "bumpy trek" of life. In this second book, entitled ***Mostly True II: Episodes,*** expect more outlandish situations based on actual experiences, humorously presented with a twist of Magical Realism. Funny Ha-Ha with a lot of Funny Peculiar mixed in. Enjoy the ride!

In ***Breathless***, a young and carefree child of four, who frolics with the neighbor's dog, finds out that four-leaf clovers don't always work as expected. The cast of characters in ***Fairytale House*** is something to write home about—if you don't live there. Greta, the Hostess with the Mostest, is confident that keeping up appearances is a good substitute for ***Seeing is Believing***. In ***Young Love*** a human tractor in high gear plows down an outgrowth of puppy love. Instead of "Baby makes three," in the story ***The Baby Maker,*** baby makes four with the addition of a meddlesome mother-in-law, a done deal. ***Civil Disobedience*** is about the price a middle-class house wife, a young mother, pays when she challenges the status quo. The ***Dinner Show*** is a madcap courtroom happening, like something out of a Fellini film. ***The Glimpse***, a mother and daughter's reunion reveals how fickle fate can be. When ***Opportunity Knocks,*** a woman ditches her unsavory past for a new beginning in Paradise. A Zen Meditation Center is where a confused woman goes to figure out her life and learns how to ***Dance in the Void***. In ***The Light Fantastic,*** a dancer is taught a way to gracefully rebound after years of falling and feeling stuck.

Breathless

Buoyant and free as a butterfly, four-year-old Linda flutters and swirls around the perimeter of her ranch-style house with her dance partner, Trigger Bee, the neighbor's energized brown and black spotted dog. Linda's long, blonde hair flies in the wind and sparkles in the warm Las Vegas sun. After several rounds, the graceful pair alights onto a patch of lush green clover, under a rustling willow tree. "Look, Trigger Bee, here is a clover with four leaves. That's a lucky one," Linda says, placing the clover carefully in the pocket of her red shorts as the panting dog rests his head on her knee and watches. Looking into his gentle brown eyes, she asks, "Trigger Bee, do you like my hair? Aunt Polly braided it, you know. Aunt Polly says that I am a beautiful princess. I know, *you* can be my handsome prince. Prince Trigger." Trigger Bee thumps his long tail on the ground. "Okay, time to dance again." As Linda jumps up, so does Trigger Bee, wagging his tail. Linda tears off some low-hanging willow branches, and places them on the dog's head. "We walk in a circle for this one. *A-tisket, a-tasket, a gr...*Oh, silly prince, you dropped your crown." She carefully replaces the branches on the dog's head, wrapping the leaves around his floppy ears. Then she continues singing, *"...a green and yellow...."* When the song ends, Linda says, "Very good, Prince Trigger Bee! Now, we will do your favorite, *Ring around the Rosie*. Linda raises her arms up and Trigger Bee vaults into the air as she catches his front paws. As they tip-toe in a circle, Linda sings, *"Ring around the Rosie"*. After the song, they tumble onto the ground below an open window. Triple digits have not yet marked the summer in Sin City, but things are already heating up inside the house. Harsh phrases exchanged between Linda's parents pierce the air and land heavily on the carefree playmates below.

"You did what with your paycheck?" Mother shouts.

"I placed it on a winning horse. He was supposed to win, all the…."

"On a horse? You bet the whole paycheck on a horse?"

"He usually places first."

"Usually! What good is usually? Huh? You fool."

"I didn't want to come to Vegas. Everyone back east warned us against this place".

"Everyone? Like your mother, you mean?"

"Las Vegas has a bad reputation. Lots of people fall into gambling out here."

"Fall into, huh? Reputation? Ha! Ha! Sounds like your Mother, all right. All she ever thinks about is reputation. Even I didn't have a reputation that was good enough for her son, did I?"

"If you hadn't followed your sister Polly out here, everything would have been just fine."

"Oh, so now it's my fault; is it?" Mother coughs and wheezes. "Mama's boy. Why don't you just go home to Mama? Quick, get me the asthma powder…put it on the lid and light it!"

Linda cries. Trigger Bee whines softly and licks her tears. She takes Trigger Bee's head in her hands and looks into her dear friend's eyes. "Time to go home, Trigger." Trigger Bee whines and slowly wags his long skinny tail before it droops down. She hugs him and walks him to his gate. Trigger Bee goes sadly through the gate with his head down.

In the darkened house, the atmosphere is laden with smoke from the burning asthma powder. Linda coughs as she enters the somber environment, where Brother Norman and her father sit huddled at the dining room table. A stream of light and fumes filter through the bathroom door, left ajar. Linda sits down next to Norman.

"Norman, what's wrong with Mommy?"

"She is trying to catch her breath. Sssh."

To Linda, Norman's face looks like a tied up knot. Her father's chin sags. Linda coughs some more; the smoke is getting to her. The bathroom door slaps open and Mother appears in the hallway, her face locked in a snarl. Her eyes glare and then glaze over as she looks in the direction of her husband. Linda sees a small flame curl out of her mother's nose. Shaking, Linda reaches in her pocket and wraps her hand around a wilted clover.

The small curl of a flame erupts into a massive blaze that sends Linda's scorched father all the way back to Maryland, into the safety net of his mother's arms.

The next morning, Linda and Trigger Bee dance again. It's a morning date, every day. When Linda finds a new four leaf clover, she tells Trigger Bee, "This one is for you, because I am lucky to have you for a friend." Trigger Bee licks her face and they dance happily around the yard.

Fairytale House

"Fairytales can come true; it can happen to you"....**Lookout!**
~ from Young at Heart, song by Doug Hulstine.

Looking back, Regina realized that the house she grew up in looked like it came out of a fairytale. It resembled a castle with arched portals, decorative turrets, and a gray thatched roof … and it was inhabited by elves, fairy godmothers, and a dragon. From the ordinary perspective, it was just a house with renters; but, Regina lived there, so she knew its mythical potential.

Regina's mother, Rita, had no education or work experience, but she could sell you the shirt off your own back. She was clever, feisty, and a single mom with two children to raise. To break even, she had walls put up to divide the large chambers and convert the carriage house into 2 chambers. When all were painted and furnished, she advertised for roomers. The real estate lady told her that a real movie star once lived there. Who could resist an ad that said: 'Live in a Movie Star Castle. Luxurious Chambers with full Pantry and Cooking privileges. Your home away from home. Only $15 a month."

Among those who took up residence in the Castle was Joe, whom Regina and her brother Steven called "The Little Ole Magic Elf". He had a wrinkled face and a straggly beard. They were sure that he must have been a magic act in which he consumed flaming swords, because he didn't even burn himself on the hot skillet when he made eggs disappear out of the frying pan without ever touching a plate. Regina sat right next to him and marveled as he gulped his food. She didn't see him chew it: she was sure that he swallowed it whole.

Lester, a scrawny guy, who never came out of his room, was "The Shrunken-up Hermit Elf". Rita banished him with his collection of empty spirit bottles which he stashed under his bed. Rita expected her tenants to be sociable; standoffish types, especially spirited ones, were not welcome.

"The Crooner Elf," a robust individual with the chest of an opera singer, sang in a cocktail lounge until the wee hours of the morning. He sported a black wavy pompadour like The Great Caruso. One night, Regina and her brother Steven put cracker crumbs in between "The Crooner Elf's" sheets before he came home. He bellowed and hit all the high notes the next day, when he announced, "Is this how you show respect for a star? I will not live in such a place!" Regina and Steven stood off to the side and giggled at his lyrical outburst.

With "The Shrunken-up Hermit Elf" and the "The Crooner Elf" off the premises, Rita ranted and raved, "How am I going to pay my bills now?" Overwhelmed, she glared at her two responsibilities. She threw a shoe at Steven, who dared to laugh. "You think it's funny, huh?"

After observing Rita frowning at her checkbook trying to make ends meet, Steven sensed that the Dragon Lady would be arriving in the near future, and informed Regina.

"Really?" Regina replied. "Do dragons bite?"

"Maybe. Depends on how mad they get."

"Oh! How can you tell if they are mad?"

"That will be obvious. Their nostrils will flare, their eyes will bulge, and flames will fly out of their mouths." Steven twisted up his face and pretended to shoot flames out of his mouth, spitting in every direction.

"Eick! that's horrible," Regina responded, brushing off the spit.

"You don't want to be around when they are mad. It's best to hide if you see one get angry."

"Hide? Hide where?"

"In the bathroom, and lock the door to be safe."

"I will, I certainly will."

"Beware, you never know with dragons. They can be singing a sweet song and doing a jolly dance one moment, and then suddenly flare at you without warning. When you see her arrive, be ready to run to the bathroom and lock the door."

Not being able to depend on a full rooming house for income, Rita opened the Young Elves Nursery School in the hinterland behind the castle. Regina enjoyed the nursery rhymes that her mother sang and danced with the children, including her. Her favorite rhyme was about a girl with a curl in the middle of her forehead. The girl could be good or very bad.

A few days later, loud music from the Parlor made Regina and Steven look up from their Monopoly game. Rita had put on a record and was dancing the Charleston. Her legs were flying in every direction and knocking over furniture. They went to take a closer look, at which point Rita's foot slammed into Regina's shin. Regina ran crying to the bathroom and put her leg under the cold water of the bathtub faucet. When she returned, Rita sang Regina a song, a sweet one, called *When You're Smiling* to get Regina to stop crying.

With Rita focused on Regina, Steven began edging towards the bathroom. Suddenly, Rita turned the Charleston music back on, kicked away a throw rug, and began to strut her stuff again. She grabbed the broom leaning against the wall to be her partner. Steven shouted in Regina's ear before he dashed to the bathroom, "The Dragon Lady has arrived and she is mad."

"Where?"

"Right there, where Mother was."

Regina stood at the doorway of the Parlor looking for her mother. The Charleston music was louder. Mother was gone; in her place was a creature, The Dragon Lady. The creature was flailing around the room, disorientated, swinging the broom. Its nostrils were flaring, its eyes were bulging, and flames flew out of its mouth. Regina watched as the broom transformed into a slapping heavy tail. Quickly, she turned and raced back down the hallway to the bathroom door and yanked on the doorknob. The door was locked. She rattled the handle, nervously.

"Steven, let me in! Unlock the door! Quick!"

The dragon closed in on Regina, ready to attack.

Regina pleaded with the dragon, "I am a good girl! I didn't do anything! Don't hit me! Ow! Ow! Stop it!"

The raging dragon didn't hear her; it flew at Regina. Flames engulfed its gigantic, scaly body. The heavy tail flapped hard on Regina's legs. The dragon's sharp claws grabbed her and held her still. It belched fire in her face.

"Bad girl! Bad girl! Always causing trouble," it snorted and howled as its tail pounded Regina's legs.

Regina sank onto the floor, screaming, "Stop! Stop! Stop! You're hurting me!" Finally, the dragon, morphing back into Rita, receded to a bedroom. In great pain, Regina looked at her legs, now covered with large black and blue bruises. Sobbing, Regina asked, "How could she do that to me? Why did she do that to me? I didn't do anything to deserve that. I am a good girl."

On weekend nights, when Rita went to the singles' dances to let off steam, Fairy Godmothers (F.G) Ellie and Ruth Love babysat young Regina. F.G. Ellie was bedridden, so the three of them stayed in their chamber all evening. The rose-clad wallpaper made the chamber seem like a Royal Garden. What happened in that Garden spanned time and space.

"It was them Injuns you had to watch for," F.G. Ellie related. "You never knew if they were just 'round the bend. We kept our oxen in good shape, in case we had to make a run for it. When we'd see them painted faces peeking out behind a boulder, we'd give them cows a slap to get 'em goin'. Whoo! Whee! Off we'd travel, the coach aswayin' and abumpin' over them prairie rocks. Why, that was back in the 1870s. I was about your age then, Miss Reggie."

Regina loved to sit beside by F.G. Ellie's pallet as she told stories of crossing the plains in a covered wagon. "Boy, oh boy! I wish I could have been there. That sounds exciting."

"Yes, honey. It was thrillin', you bet!" F.G. Ellie had the sweetest expression in the world; all her wrinkles and neck folds merged neatly with the folds of the blankets.

In contrast to F.G. Ellie, her sister F.G. Ruth Love Jenkins, a nurse, was stern and worldly; but "Love" was her middle name. One day, one of the nursery school elves entered the chamber with Regina to see the rose garden, and instead noticed the large chamber pot in the F.G's room. "What's that?" asked the elf.

"That's none of your business. You go tend to your knittin'," F.G Ruth Love snapped.

"I don't know how to knit," pouted the little elf.

F.G Ruth Love escorted her to the door and told her, "It's high time you learned." F.G. Ruth Love wore a starched white uniform, instead of a flowing gown like F.G. Ellie. She wore bright red lipstick, and had her wrinkles and weight under control.

From her Fairy God Mothers, Regina learned to play Canasta while listening to "Hawaii Calls" on the radio. She loved the sound of the ocean and swaying palm trees in the background.

"I'm going to go to Hawaii when I grow up," she proudly stated.

"Good for you. Hawaii is on the other side of the ocean. It is far away," said F.G. Ruth Love.

"I will be a Hula Girl."

"Sounds exciting," said F.G. Ellie.

"Yes, it will be."

F.G. Ruth Love being proper about things, showed Regina how to pray a prayer of protection before she went to sleep. Now Regina had something to do to protect herself from the Dragon Lady, who appeared on a regular basis with a curl on her forehead.

Seeing is Believing

"So remember when you tell those little white lies
that the night has a thousand eyes."
~ Bobby Vee, American singer, songwriter and musician

Greta, my mother, loved parties: the crowd, the music, the food, the games, the decorations, etc. etc. She loved them so much that she planned her pregnancies accordingly. My older brother Aaron and I were both born in April, just like Mother. With our three birthdays only a week apart, the annual Backyard Birthday Bash was definitely an item to calendar. And everyone on the block did just that; the more, the merrier for Greta, who called herself the "Hostess with the Mostest."

Making everything look good was very important to Greta, whatever the occasion might be. At the 3rd annual Bash, Aaron mentioned that one of the picnic tables was flaking. She responded, "Throw something over it. No one needs to see that. We'll use all the tables we've got."

Concerned, I added, "But the bench part is full of splinters."

"I don't know. I don't care. It will be too dark to see the seats anyway. Don't make a scene, Lisa. Be a good girl, now."

For Mother, "no one has to see" included undesirable people, like her sister Karen's back-east boyfriend, Pete. Aunt Karen had just married Frank. He was well off; he owned a corner grocery store. Mother introduced them; Frank was her best friend's brother. "Forget the guy back east. No one needs to see him," Mother told Aunt Karen. But Aunt Karen didn't love Frank; she still loved Pete.

Aunt Karen was a beautician. She liked to fix up my hair and dress me up in her own pretty clothes. I am big for 8 and Aunt Karen was petite, so her clothes fit me perfectly and they are so pretty, just like Aunt Karen was. I loved Aunt Karen. Aunt Karen never said "no one has to see."

Last week, Mother and Aunt Karen argued loudly in the living room. I heard them from my room. "I am not happy with him! I am going to divorce Frank."

"That's stupid! You can't do that. That's the stupidest thing I've ever heard," Mother snapped, bawling out her kid sister.

"I don't love him. I know that now. After seeing Pete again, I know I want to be with him."

"You didn't need to see him. Love, schmuf. He doesn't have a pot to pee in. You don't need to see him again. No one has to know about him. Don't think about him, that's all."

"That's not all."

The argument got more heated, turning into a shouting match.

"I think about him. I know he is the one for me!" Aunt Karen pleaded.

Mother stamped her foot. "Don't be a fool. You're talking nonsense! Frank has a business! He can support you."

"You never take me seriously, do you? You don't give a damn about what matters to me. You never have."

"What? That's ridiculous. Look what you're trying to do now ... ruin your future. Believe me, I know what's best for you."

"You know what's best! Ha! I don't see you happily married! I don't see you married at all!"

"That has nothing to do with it. You think it is easy making do alone? Quit acting like a child!"

"I am not a child! Quit treating me like one, you bitch."

"What? What, what did you call me?" Mother screamed.

"Bitch. That is what you are and always have been!"

"The nerve! You talk to your older sister like that? Get out of here. Get out of my house and don't come back. I don't want to see you until you come to your senses."

"Don't worry! You won't be seeing me again."

Mother called Aunt Karen the next day. She didn't answer her phone. We went to her apartment and knocked on her door, several times. When she didn't answer, we peered through a small window in the door. Aunt Karen's body was strewn on the floor in a pool of blood.

"What is all that blood from?" I wanted to know.

"Aunt Karen has her period."

"What's a period?"

Aunt Karen had slit her wrists. She was only 33. Mother closed the curtain on the small window. "Just forget it. You didn't see anything."

As the sun set, people arrived at The Birthday Bash. By now, Mother was busy greeting the guests. In her excitement, you could hear her shout, "Hoo! Ha!" as the neighbors poured in from up and down the block, carrying presents and food.

People of all ages ran, jumped, laughed, and played in our big grassy backyard. The highlight of the evening was a stumble through rotten apricots to Pin the Tail on the Donkey. The whole yard was filled with the fragrance of over-ripe fruit. As the blind-folded person made his or her way in the direction of the picture of the donkey, they squished the fallen apricots with their bare feet. Everyone laughed as the blinded person slipped and regained balance through the slush.

As evening wore on, Mother entertained everyone with dances and slightly scary stories. Mother loved being in the spotlight. She was a one-woman show. Everyone had a great time; everyone except Aunt Karen.

After most of the guests left, Mother, exhausted from all the excitement, flopped down on the splintered bench. "Ouch!" She jumped up with a splinter lodged in her thigh. When the few remaining people turned to look at her, she smiled. No one had to see her upset at this joyous event. She had to wait until the next day to visit the doctor. By then, the wound was infected. Even after the doctor removed the sliver of wood, the pierced area turned into a chronic boil. Whenever she sat down, you could hear her say, "I am my own worst enemy."

"No one saw" Aunt Karen anymore, except for me. I saw her every night, laughing through my bedroom window.

Young Love

"Life is what happens when you're busy making other plans."
~ John Lennon and others

One day when Janie comes home from junior high school, there is an unfamiliar woman and man in her kitchen. The 50ish woman is wearing a man's sport shirt, peddle-pushers, and an apron, while cooking fried chicken. A man, short and stout like a tractor, about 30 is sitting at her breakfast nook table, reading the sports' page. They have made themselves at home, these two strangers.

"Are you a Princess?" asks the woman. The man looks up from the newspaper and shoots her a wink.

Janie is astonished. *Are they talking to me? The only princesses I know are in storybooks or in the movies. And who are they, anyway?*

"I'm just a real life girl."

"But you are as pretty as a princess," the woman says.

"Thank you. Who are you, anyway? What are you doing here?"

"We live here, moved in just this mornin'. I'm Jenny and this here is my son, Tommy. He's going to be a lawyer."

"Oh, you're renting a room? I thought Mother wasn't doing that anymore, since she got married."

"Your mother is married? I didn't meet a husband."

"Well, she was married; but, she got divorced again."

The succulent aroma from the frying chicken makes Janie's stomach growl.

"Usually, no one is here when I get home."

"Oh...that's sad," says Jenny.

"We've rented the large room near the kitchen," Tommy states.

"Oh."

"Pleased to meet you, Princess. What is your name?"

"I am Janie."

"You are very polite, Janie." Jenny winks and nods her head towards her son.

"Thank you, but I am really **not a princess**, just a regular girl."

"You can be our princess. And we will always be here to greet you, when you come home from school, with a nice home cooked meal."

"Really? You're kidding. I mean, that would be highly unusual, but nice."

"And so are you. And you are a very pretty princess. When does your mother get home from work?"

"I'm not sure. Maybe in a little while."

"Would you like to have dinner with us, Princess Janie?"

"**Real** fried chicken, not the TV dinner kind? Smells good."

Tommy chimes in, "You bet. Mom's the 'best cook in the county.' That's what they always said back in Nebraska."

"Nebraska, that's far away, isn't it?"

"Half-way across the country. Come sit down. Right here," Tommy says, as he moves his bulky body a couple of inches and pats the place next to him. He taps his foot nervously; inside his motor is starting to rev.

Janie is very hungry, and who knows when her mother will be getting home? Maybe she's working late again. Rather than grab leftovers or a TV dinner from the icebox, she accepts the invitation. As her nose and growling stomach take over, she sits next to Tommy. His heavy leg feels like a huge tire against hers. The whole thing feels a little weird to her, but she doesn't know why. "You're wearing a uniform."

"I am in the Army…intelligence."

"But you live here. That doesn't make sense if you are in the Army."

"I am in the Army. But, they allow me to live at home to take care of Mom."

"Take care of her? Is she sick?"

"No, but I am the Man of the House. My father died."

"My brother and I don't have a father either, and my mother doesn't have a husband. So, I guess we don't have 'a Man of the House.'"

"I'll just have to be 'the Man of the House' for all of you."

"Huh?"

"Don't worry. My boy has a high IQ. He figures things out for people," Jenny quickly changes the subject.

"Best chicken you'll ever eat," Tommy adds.

Jenny sits down right next to Janie on the other side, and Tommy moves in closer. She is wedged between them. They might even appear to be a happy family of three, to a passerby. Of course, there was no one passing by in the kitchen, but Janie felt self-conscious and crammed in.

"What grade are you?" Tommy asks.

"I just started 7th grade. I am 13."

"Ha. Really? Only 13? You look a lot older than that." He grins, glances at her developed breasts, and winks again.

* * *

In the days following, Janie enjoys the attention of Tommy and Jenny. She seems to be the sole object of their attention. Tom and Jenny are always happy to see her when she gets home from school. Tom always has a little present for her, like a scarf, or some perfume, or a barrette. Jenny teaches her how to iron clothes and cook. She treats her like her own daughter. With Janie's mother gone most of the time, they are a makeshift little family unit.

Janie wants to know more about them. Curious, she asks, "Jenny, where is your husband?"

Jenny clears her throat and gives a short answer to that question. "I married a man from Omaha when I was real young. We divorced before Tommy was born."

"You never even saw your father, Tommy?"

"No, I never did. But Mr. Bill, the Mayor, was like a father to me."

"Really, the Mayor was like your father? That's something!"

"We lived with him in a mansion. Someday, I'm going to be rich, and belong to a country club just like Mr. Bill, when I am an attorney."

"Wow! That's terrific! I think that you would be a very good attorney."

"Why, thank you, Janie," Tommy says, putting his arm around her. "Being an attorney is a hard job, takes a lot of sacrifice. But, it a stable profession and profitable, to boot."

"I am proud of my boy, you bet, Honey. He is very good with people, and ambitious."

"But, I thought you were in the Army. Isn't that your job?"

"Oh, that's just temporary. I'll be done with my service to the country in a few years."

"And then what?"

"Then I'll go to law school to become an attorney."

"Wow, you **are** ambitious. Sounds like a lot of work, going to school for it and everything."

"There is a lot to it. But, once I make my mind up about something, I go for it," he says with a big smile, a large wink and a grunt.

One day when Tommy is in another room, Janie notices a picture of a woman on Tommy's dresser, and asks, "Who's that?"

"Oh, that's a girl from back home. Her name is Elaine," Jenny grumbles. "That one's been around a few corners, you can be sure of that," Jenny slurs out the side of her mouth.

It doesn't sound like Jenny likes Elaine very much. I wonder what she means by "a few corners?" I turn a few corners every day, on my way to school.

Janie has a delicious dinner with Jenny and Tom every night. While she does the dishes, Tom asks Janie a lot of questions, like: "Do you like school? Do have a boyfriend?" He wants to know everything that she thinks and feels. She enjoys the attention and interest that he shows in her.

She surprises the heck out of him when she answers, "I am in love with Billy. We go steady. Billy is so sweet and really cute. He is my forever guy. We're going to be married someday." A truly gallant lad, Billy walks her home every day, carrying her school books. After a lingering goodbye kiss, Janie floats into the house.

Janie doesn't know anything about Sugar Daddies. She certainly doesn't know that she has one. Janie sees Tommy just as a good and caring friend, not as a mate. He gives her things that her mother won't buy for her, and is a reliable shoulder to cry on when she has a bad day.

Tommy is insatiable. Day after day, he watches Billy kissing Janie goodbye. He yearns for a taste of those young lips. He's convinced that he's earned it, after all he's given her. One day, he gears up to claim his sweet treat. When she enters the house, he greets her. "Janie, I have a special present for you today. It's in the dining room."

"Oh, it must be the matching angora socks and sweater that I told you about, the one all the other girls are wearing." She innocently follows him into the dining room.

"It's a surprise now. You have to sit down and close your eyes."

Janie does as instructed. With great expectation, she sits and squeezes her eyes shut. She can't wait to see and feel that soft fuzzy sweater with the matching socks. *I wonder what color they will be.*

Tommy quietly pulls a chair right up against Janie's, wraps his arm around her, and draws her very close. When she opens her eyes, his face is one inch away. In high gear, with his lips pursed and breathing heavily, he tells Janie, "Show me how you kiss your boyfriends, Janie,"

"What? Where's my present?"

"It's coming. Be patient. Just a little kiss first for an old friend."

"But, I don't love you. I love Billy."

"That doesn't matter. Just show me how you kiss Billy. I've been good to you, haven't I?"

"Yes, but…," Before she knows what hits her, the tractor makes contact, the kiss happens. Just like that, it is over. She runs to the bathroom and washes her face and rubs her lips extra hard. *How could he do that to me? I would tell Mother on him; but, she never listens to anything I say. She'll pretend that she doesn't hear or she's busy, or just laugh it off.*

As the months pass, Janie spends more time with Billy. Tommy decides that he has to do something before she goes too far with Billy and the boy takes over his territory. So, he revs up his motor to go in for the plow. He hires a friend of Janie's older brother, Manny, a wise-ass who will do just about anything for money. He gives Manny a call. "Hey, Manny, how's it going? Good, glad to hear it. Say, Manny, I've got a deal for you, a real good deal. How much? One hundred bucks, plus gas and other travel expenses. No, no, I don't want you to murder somebody. Just take ole Billy, Janie's boyfriend, for a good time in Vegas. Yeah, a good time. You know what I mean, now, don't ya? It's a deal then, right? Good. I knew I could depend on you."

Manny makes sure Billy gets what every teenage boy wets the bed for every night: SEX, FULL ON SEX. He also throws in a bit of free mature friend advice, "Stick with younger chicks. Those your age end up running your life." Billy doesn't question the guidance of an older and wiser guy who had shown him the time of his life. In no uncertain terms, Billy has an unforgettable time, one that changes his and Janie's life.

One day, Janie notices Manny's souped-up 1956 Chevy arrive in front of her house. Manny keeps the motor running as Billy hops out, walks to front door and rings the doorbell. Janie opens the door and gives Billy a big hug and pulls him inside. "I've been trying to call you! Where have you been? You look tired."

"I just got in from Vegas ... with Manny. Yeah, I didn't get any sleep last couple of nights."

"Vegas? With Manny? Manny, my brother's friend? That jerk?"

"Yeah, he's waiting for me in the car."

Janie pulls the curtain back. Outside, she sees Tommy and Manny standing by the car. Tommy, with a big grin, pats Manny on the shoulder and shakes his hand. Tommy hands Manny some cash. *Wonder why Tom is giving Manny money.*

"I just dropped by to say it's over between us."

"WHAT? What do you mean?"

"I'm a different person now."

"You look the same. What's going on? We love each other."

"I got laid in Vegas."

"You got what?"

"I gotta go. Manny is waiting. I don't want to hurt you anymore. I wouldn't be satisfied with just kissing anymore."

"It's okay. We can do it. I love you. You love me. We are going to get married later."

"Maybe not. No, I couldn't do that to you. What if you got pregnant? It would never work now. What we had was just puppy love. You'll get over it." Billy heads for the door.

"Wait…. No, Billy! I will always love you."

Billy walks out. Janie goes to the window to watch Billy go to the car and nod to Tommy. Manny, who is smoking a cigarette, gives a lighted one to Billy, and they get back in the car and speed off. Tommy picks up his suitcase and walks to the front door, a happy man. He has a big smile when he enters the house. Janie rushes to him, and falls against him in tears.

"Hey, hey! What's going on, Princess?" Tommy asks, waiting for the good news.

"Billy broke up with me! He doesn't love me anymore!" Janie cries. Tommy dries her tears with his handkerchief.

"Now, now. You are a beautiful young woman. The right one will come along. Now, gimme a big smile."

Janie sits down on the couch and barely smiles. "How's law school and your apartment?" she asks, with little interest.

"It's nice. Getting good grades, and the apartment is fine, close to the Law school. Convenient. You'll have to come visit sometime."

"How are your classes? Hard?"

"Yep. Real hard. Study all the time."

"You'll be a good attorney. We have a new Roomer. His name is Harry."

"Oh, yeah? What's he do?"

"He watches TV all day. He's old. He doesn't work anymore. He was a graphic artist. Sometimes he helps me with my homework."

"Helps you? How?"

"With my lettering. He has such sad eyes."

"Make sure he keeps his hands to himself."

"Like I said, he's an old man."

"I brought you a little present." He hands it to her. Janie opens it. It is an autograph hound. She gives Tommy a big hug.

"Everyone has one, except me."

"Now you have one, too. Mom thought you'd like it. She just got them in the store."

"Oh, the drug store. How's she doing there?"

"Real well. Real well. And it's making enough to put me through Law School."

"That's great! Give her my love."

"Will do. She said to bring you up sometime for a visit."

"Yes, that would be nice."

That evening, Tommy sleeps on the couch. Janie hears him call her name, gets out of bed, and goes to the living room. Tommy lounges on the couch in his boxer shorts. He smiles as she enters the room, reaches through the slit in his shorts and jacks off. Embarrassed and confused, Janie goes back to her room.

Before Tommy leaves the next morning, he tells Janie, "Remember to keep your id hid. I'll be able to tell by looking at you, if you don't. Hee, hee, hee. Be good now, and save it for me."

He closes the suitcase and sets it on the floor, ready to go.

"What in the world are you talking about? What is an 'id'?"

Tommy laughs and walks out the door.

* * *

In the next year, Janie's relationship with her mother grows progressively worse. Harry, the old man in the back room, tries to kiss her after a teaching session.

"He's just a lonely old man. Take it worth a grain of salt. You're too sensitive. Without his rent money, I can't make ends meet," her mother says.

"It's not just the old man. Your snoring keeps me awake. I want you to ask him to move, and give me that room to myself!"

"I told you already, I can't afford it. Don't make trouble."

Later, she hears her mother complain to one of her male friends, in the living room. "The kid has been acting up again. I need to put a stop to it. I don't know what I'm going to do with her. I have bills to pay. She wants me to tell my one and only roomer to move because he asked her for a little kiss. He's just a lonely old man. He didn't mean any harm. But she is making a big deal out of it, like she always does. I don't know what I'm going to do with her. I need that money."

"Leave it to me. I'll beat some sense into her," says the friend.

When Janie hears this she decides to run away. She grabs a few clothes and lowers herself out of the bedroom window. Clear of the house, she runs to a phone booth and calls Tommy. "It's me, Janie. He's going to beat me up."

"Now, calm down. Get a hold of yourself. Who's going to beat you up?"

"My Mother's big, fat, mean friend."

"Now, now; don't worry. Where are you? I'll come and get you right away."

"I'm at Pico and Robertson, in the phone booth by Albertson's."

When Tommy arrives, he gives her a comforting hug, and nudges her into the front seat of his car. She cries all the way to his apartment. At his apartment, after he gives her a comforting cup of hot chocolate, he tickles her. "Stop that! I don't like to be tickled." He giggles and keeps tickling her. She gets up, but he chases her around the room. She runs into the bedroom and locks the door.

The next morning, Janie asks, "Why did you tickle and chase me last night?"

"Oh, you were so sad. I just wanted to cheer you up."

"Oh, was that it. Okay." Janie believes him.

As usual, Janie complains to Tommy about her mother. "I want my own room at home. My mother snores up a storm, and that old man didn't keep his hands to himself."

"He didn't, huh? He will have to move out. I will see to it. She should give you your own room. You are a young lady now."

"I know, but she says she can't afford it."

"Get a part-time job and pay your mother for the room."

"You have to be 16 to get a job at the theater. That's what I'd like to do, be an usherette, like some of my friends."

"You don't have to be 16. Just say you are."

"Really? I can do that?"

"Try it. It won't be hard for you to lie about your age. You look older than your age. You can get away with it."

"Okay. I will."

"I'll talk to your mother about it, and we'll see that you get your own room."

"Oh, I sure would appreciate that. I can never talk to her. She doesn't listen to me."

"She never has. Don't worry. I'll take care of it."

* * *

The theater manager, where Janie gets a job as an usherette, has a shiny bald head and looks like Mr. Magoo, the cartoon character. Before the show and during intermission, as the throng of theatergoers mingles and read posters of upcoming movies, they reach in their pockets for a cigarette or something and usually drop a few coins. After the audience goes to sit inside the theater for the show, Janie laughs as she watches that shiny bald head flash as he scans the ground for change.

Magoo's behavior outside is funny; but, inside, he scares Janie. Once he closes the office door, he chases her around the desk. "Do you want your paycheck, hum? Janie? Hum?" murmurs old Magoo, grinning from ear to ear. He rants and raves around the room every Friday before handing over her paycheck. Fortunately, he is only half-serious, a clown at best.

She gets to the theater at the same time every day, and always sees the same part of the movie *South Pacific*, set in Hawaii, in which Bloody Mary sings the song "Happy Talk." After being chased around a desk for her paycheck and singing "Happy Talk" in her sleep for weeks, she finds a new usherette job. In the new job, she has to smile all the time when she is stationed in front of the theater doors, even when no one was around. The smile feels pasted on her. When she isn't working, she finds herself smiling like a goon. People think that she is laughing at them… and smirk back at her.

She is not fond of her job, but it pays the rent and gives her some privacy. It is worth working to have her own space. But, she doesn't have enough left over for clothes. When she asks her mother for some new clothes, she hears, "Money doesn't grow on trees. How many times do I have to tell you that? Don't make me repeat myself!"

"Right, you've told me before. Nice dresses you bought for yourself! Nice nails!"

"Why don't you stop? It doesn't matter about you. It's just too bad about you, isn't it? Are you the Complaint Department? You want to go to the Juvenile Delinquent home?"

Janie seethes.

"You're too sensitive. Ha, ha, ha. You're so abused," her mother adds.

"I am not too sensitive. But you *are* abusive," Janie counters.

"You don't have a roof over your head?"

"I pay for that!"

"Big shot! You don't have food to eat? Everyone should be as lucky as you. I never had it so easy."

It is endless, this bickering, and it gets even worse. They quarrel on the day Janie leaves home to take a mother's aid job near UCLA, where she is to attend college. They had planned a "good-bye" dinner party. Janie has been waiting forever for her mother to come home.

At 8:00 P.M, when she finally arrives, Janie scowls. "It's kind of late for dinner, isn't it?"

"Dinner? What? You didn't eat yet? I left lamb chops in the fridge."

"This is the day that I am leaving for college. You said we would have a good-bye dinner."

"So, kill me! Big deal, great big deal, so what? There you go making something out of nothing again! Bernie needed a pair of shoes for work tomorrow." Bernie is husband number 4. "You are too sensitive. Bernie needed a pair of shoes; they were on sale. Too bad about you! You only think of yourself. Why don't you to bang your head against the wall?"

Too sensitive, too sensitive, too sensitive; she is totally insensitive. "You've never been there when I needed you."

"What, I didn't raise you? It wasn't easy, you know. I had to make ends meet. Others had it worse. You should be grateful!"

Ends meet, ends meet, ends meet; they have met. "Grateful! For what? For a mother who mistreats and ignores me!" Janie lifts her arm and slaps her mother's face.

"I'm sorry I ever had you!" her mother says.

"Obviously! I've always known that." Janie walks out the door, letting the door slam behind her. *I have had enough of this woman; she won't hurt me again.*

The mother's aid job doesn't work out, and Janie's grades plummet. She drops out of college and has nowhere to go… except to Tommy. As usual, he is always there for her.

Tommy picks her up. Back at his apartment, he chases her again, and this time he lands with her on the couch. He sits close to her and puts his arm around her. She starts to cry.

Tommy claps his hands loudly. Janie looks around and can't figure out why he does that.

"Now, now! Everything is going to be all right," he says, gently patting her on the shoulder. Suddenly, Janie sits up when she hears her mother's laugh coming from behind the bathroom door. "What is it, Janie?"

"It's my mother. She's in the bathroom. She is hiding there…waiting for me. She's angry at me for running away. She is out to get me."

"It's all in your mind, Janie. Just relax, now. She can't get you anymore. I'll protect you, like always." Sparked by her vulnerability, Tommy slowly unbuttons her blouse.

"What are you doing?"

"Just making you more comfortable. You are breathing heavily. I'm loosening you up a bit." By now, Tommy has unzipped his pants. He places her hand on his penis. Janie has never seen or touched a penis before. He closes his hand around hers and slides it up and down his hardening penis. Fascinated and scared all at the same time, she starts to scream. He covers her mouth and pulls her on top of him, removing her underpants and spreading her legs. "Don't worry. I'll take care of you."

"My mother, she wants to grab me and beat me up."

"Now, now, settle down. I won't let her get you. You're safe in my arms."

"What are you doing to me? Let me go. Don't do that to me! I don't want sex with you."

"Settle down now. You're not alone. We'll take it real easy, now. Just relax, now. Open up a little. It will be over soon. I won't hurt you."

When his stiff penis pierces her hymen, she screams in pain. As blood mixed with semen spills onto the couch, she vomits. With a pale face, she watches as he cleans up everything with a kitchen towel. "Here, take this. It will make you feel better. You've been through a lot." He gives her a sedative. "Like I said, you'll be fine now, just fine. Nothing to worry about. Just lay back and relax."

As Janie doses off, Tommy quietly goes to the bathroom and opens the door. The housekeeper gratefully receives her check and tiptoes to and out the front door.

The Baby Maker

"Just got back from a pleasure trip: I took my
mother-in-law to the airport."
~ Henny Youngman

There is still time to do it safely; but, Jack, her husband, won't go for it. He talks her out of it. He is good at doing that; he just pulls on the guilt thread that her mother stitched into her.

"I am not happy being married to you. We are not right for each other, Jack. I don't want to bring a child into this unsuitable relationship. I want an abortion".

"Unsuitable? Abortion? What's gotten into you? I love you. You married me, and now you want a divorce? You're just like your mother!"

"I am not like my mother! No, I'm not!"

"Think things over, Rena. Don't make a hasty decision. That's what your mother would do. Getting married and divorced is just like crossing the street for her."

"Yes, I guess that's true. Okay, I'll think it over." Jack has the power and cleverness to make her succumb to his will, and she doesn't have the courage to trust her own decisions. He always makes sense.

"You just need to try a little harder to be happy, and let things work out. Give it some time." Rena is duped into thinking that maybe it will work, if she aims higher. No way she wants to be like her mother!

A while passes. Too dangerous now for Rena and her developing baby to have an abortion. Every morning, she vomits. Lynette, his mother, adds to the mix for disaster. They are in business together in the town where she lives. She runs the drugstore that he owns. Jack and Rena go to his mother's house every weekend, after Rena drives to L.A. during the week to buy knickknacks for the store. She travels and works too hard for a pregnant woman; she becomes very anemic and dull in spirit.

Walking into Lynette's kitchen one day, Rena sees mother and son in a tender embrace. They have a unique bond. *Why did I marry Jack? He was already married to his mother.* It isn't a romantic embrace, but it is intimate; certainly a more cherished one than any Rena has ever shared with Jack. Rena realizes that she is the third wheel, an insipid appendage, bearing a child for them. Her feelings and thoughts are laughed off. She is fed, clothed, told what to do, hushed, and exhausted. She is in their clutches.

Despite the terrible marriage relationship, Rena experiences the happiest day of her life when her daughter Candy is born. She is a beautiful girl with long black hair. She comes out feet first.

In the hospital, as Rena blissfully holds and breast-feeds her baby, a nurse rips Candy out of her arms. "The specialist is here to examine the baby's heart."

"Her heart? What's wrong with her heart?"

"She lost air in the breech birth. The specialist will check for a heart murmur." The nurse takes the baby. Rena's breath is caught in her throat.

"What are they going to do to her? Will she be okay?"

The nurse leaves and reappears later.

"Is she okay? Where is she? Bring her back to me. What are they doing to her?"

"She's fine. She is in the nursery, sleeping."

"No, bring Candy to me, now. I want my baby. I need my baby."

"You and the baby must rest now."

When Rena begins to cry, the nurse walks out saying, "Shush." Rena stares after her.

Lynette is there to "help-out" when Rena return home. While Rena is bursting with milk, Lynette insists on feeding the baby a bottle. When

Rena's breasts become clogged with milk, she gets a fever and has to stop nursing.

Lynette is frequently at their home now, interfering in family matters. Of course, Jack doesn't see it that way. He calls Rena "selfish" when she complains, and tries to put her on anti-depressants. *There is no way I am going to La-La Land! I have a baby to take care of. The only pill that I am more than willing to take is the new birth control pill.*

One day, Rena confronts the old woman. "I want you to stay out of our marriage."

Lynette begins to cry and moan, "I always thought that I was a good mother!" She runs into the kitchen and pulls out a butcher knife, like she is going to stab herself. Of course, Jack grabs the knife from her. She continues to play a central part in the life of her son and his child bride and baby maker.

Civil Disobedience

"It will always be a battle a day between those who want maximum change and those who want to maintain the status quo."
~ Gerry Adams, Irish Politician

It was 1966; anti-war protests filled the streets, were caught on camera, and kept journalists busy. Melissa was a college student in a small town, where she got wind of the major demonstrations going on at UCLA and other big city campuses. Complacency was not one of Melissa's virtues; she believed in justice for all, including herself. In fact, a rebellion had grown inside of her after 5 years of a repressive marriage.

One night after placing Corrine, her 2-year old, in her crib, she walked down the hall to the den and sat on the couch. Her obese balding husband Dan, with his fat splayed out on his chartreuse Lazy Boy, was watching TV and slugging beer. Dan prided himself on being a doctor, despite his unhealthy lifestyle. On the television, they watched a Special depicting Martin Luther King Jr.'s March on Washington, the assassination of President Kennedy, and protests against the mass murdering of civilian Vietnamese.

"What a shame! What is this show called?" asked Melissa.

"It's called 'The Peace Movement.' Some big joke, eh?"

"What do you mean 'joke'?"

"Does that mob of black faces look peaceful to you?"

"Doctor King and his followers are making a statement."

"What do you know about making statements?"

"More than you think."

"Just a Commie uprising."

"That can't be true! Martin Luther King is fighting for the civil rights of African Americans."

"You don't know anything."

"It is so sad that Kennedy had to die."

"It was necessary. Otherwise, our country would be led by Reds."

"President Kennedy was a dynamic leader. He cared about people."

"He was a Commie. He deserved what he got."

"No, he wasn't! He was a Humanitarian."

"You don't know anything. Don't worry your pretty little head about it. The Pinkos have been taken care of, and replaced by good upright citizens." Dan gobbled a fistful of salted nuts, downed a mug of beer, and wiped his palm on his shirt.

"I can read, you know!"

"You can't believe anything you read. The reporters are Commies too. Pure propaganda, that's what you read in the paper these days!" Dan turned the bag of cashews upside down, emptied the contents into his mouth, pulled up his pant leg, and scratched a perpetual huge patch of dry, red skin.

Melissa stared at him in disgust, as if she is seeing him for the first time. He resembled a hippopotamus wallowing in mud.

Scenes of the Viet Nam war flashed on the screen. "Look at all the women and babies that are being massacred!" Melissa cried out. "That's horrible!"

"Unavoidable. A necessary part of our United States army protecting our country." The hippo patted his hairy belly that stuck out through his tightly buttoned, striped nylon sport shirt. He wore it every day after work. It was tight, just like his brain. "Nothing can be done about that." The hippo let out a huge belch.

"Nothing? Our country doesn't need protecting. The country of Viet Nam is the one that needs protection!"

"That's crazy talk. You sound like one of the Commies! You are a doctor's wife with a nice home and child. That is no concern of yours."

Melissa picked up the book a friend gave her recently. After reading for a while, she turned in Dan's direction and read aloud from the book: "We can no longer ignore that voice within women that says: 'I want something more than my husband and my children and my home'."

"What? What did I hear you say?"

Melissa repeated it louder, staring straight at him. "'We can no longer ignore that voice within women that says I want something more than my husband and my children and my home'."

The hippo sloshed and surged forward, rocking the recliner and spilling his beer on the laminate floor. The Lazy Boy recliner snapped into an upright position. "What's that trash you're reading?"

Melissa held up the cover in his face. "It's called *The Feminine Mystic* by Betty Freidan. This book that has started a new movement."

Dan gapes at the cover of the book and then at Melissa. "What new movement?"

"The Feminist Movement."

Pushing the chair back to the recline position, he grunts and bellows, "Ha! You're even in the wrong decade! 'The Movement,' as you call it, happened back in the '20s or you wouldn't have the right to vote. Pure communist propaganda! Throw it away! You should spend your time reading your Dr. Spock book, like a good mother."

"I read it. I won't throw away this new book. It speaks to me."

"Speaks to you? What does that mean? It is not a talking book."

"Listen to this from NOW."

"Now what? What is all this gibberish?"

"NOW is the National Organization of Women, recently formed."

She read aloud: "'In the interests of the human dignity of women, we will protest, and endeavor to change, the false image of women now prevalent in the mass media, and in the texts, ceremonies, laws, and practices of our major social institutions. Such images perpetuate contempt for women by society and by women for themselves. We are similarly opposed to all policies and practices — in church, state, college, factory, or office — which, in the guise of protectiveness, not only deny opportunities but also foster in women self-denigration, dependence, and evasion of responsibility, undermine their confidence in their own abilities and foster contempt for women.'"

"Throw it away."

"I want something more than the vote."

"You're nuts! You have everything you need. We live the good life."

"No, we don't. I don't even have a typewriter."

"A typewriter! What in the world would you do with a typewriter?"

"I'd write, of course."

"Write what?"

"Stories."

"You don't know any stories. And anyway, we can't afford that right now. I just bought this house and land and your nice furs. Maybe in a couple of years. We'll play it by ear."

"But, I want to be a writer. I don't need fur wraps and collars! That's a waste, and cruel to animals."

"You are irrational. You have really lost it, this time. You are too anxious for your own good. Time for a little happy pill, eh?"

"I'm perfectly fine."

"You don't appreciate what I bought you? I need to show off my wife! I am a doctor. You are a doctor's wife; all doctor's wives wear furs to shindigs. You need furs. Be grateful for what you have. You're luckier than most women. They'd give their eye teeth for a fur."

"I don't need furs. I need a typewriter. I need to be a writer."

"You can't be a writer. You have to travel to be a writer. And you have responsibilities here, as a doctor's wife and as a mother."

"I have no identity. The local pharmacist calls me 'Mrs. Doctor.'"

Dan just laughed.

Melissa had reached a breaking point, but not the one recognized by the hippo. She was about to join the Civil Rights Movement. Time for a little travel. Peacefully protesting, Melissa neatly packed a bag with what she and Corrine would need to live with her mother in the big city. There, she would go to political rallies and NOW meetings, to give and gain support for important causes which didn't include hippo preservation.

* * *

Melissa expected to find Corrine at her mother's when she returned from a NOW meeting. Dan had not returned her. He picked her up on Friday and was supposed to return her on Sunday, as he'd done before; but he didn't.

"What do you mean he didn't bring her back?" she demanded an answer from her mother. "Were you here all day, or did you go shopping?"

Her mother glared at Melissa. "What do you take me for?"

"Just going on past history. You've never been around when it mattered."

"Oh, is that so?" Her voice got louder as she picked up on Melissa's anger. "I have told you that I always did my best."

"Right, yeah, sure. Ha!"

"What are you so upset about? She's not our child. We are Jewish, and she sings songs about Jesus."

"What? What in the hell are you talking about? How can you say such a thing? This is my baby you're talking about."

"You'll have another child."

"I have no time for your witless remarks! I need to go get my baby."

It so happened that Melissa's attorney had an airplane. Melissa boarded the skimpy 2-seater aircraft, fearing for her life as they lifted off the ground. There didn't seem to be enough separation between her and the great blue yonder. *I have to do this. I have to get my baby.*

Corrine wasn't there when they arrived. He had hid her someplace.

"Where is she?" Melissa asked Dan.

He looked down on her arrogantly, and simply stated that she was with the heart specialist.

"What? Who? Why?"

"Now, now, don't get upset yet. We're checking out her heart murmur. This is important now. You remember she was born with a heart murmur, which must be examined periodically."

"Oh, oh! Oh, my God! This is terrible. Is she okay?"

"Don't worry your pretty little head about it. It's just routine procedure."

"I want to see her. Is she up at the hospital?"

"No, she's down in Roseville with Mom so she can see the specialist there in the morning. Mom is taking good care of her."

"Oh, my God."

"There is nothing you can do now, until we get the result of the tests."

"Tests? What kind of tests?"

"Oh, just the usual, to rule out things."

"What things?"

"Heart disease, mainly."

"Oh, my God, oh, my poor baby!"

"Now, now, now, now, now. I told you, don't worry. I will let you know what the outcome is. You go back to L.A., and I will call you when I get the doctor's report."

Dejected and foiled, Melissa got back in the plane. When she didn't hear from him, she called. "Is she okay?"

"She's fine."

"Then bring her home. I have custody!"

"Oh, it's Great-Grandma's birthday, back in South Dakota, you know. She's in her 90s now, you know, and she has never seen Corrine. So Mom suggested that they take a trip back home to wish Grandma a Happy Birthday, you know."

"I don't know any of that, at all. What? You can't just do that! I have custody. You are breaking the law."

"Law! Now, don't be selfish. That's very unattractive."

"Oh, the nerve, you asshole!"

"Well, I have to go now. I have patients to see. Take care, my dear."

Dinner Show

"People love scandal; people love drama. They love strip-
ping away the layers to see what's really in there, and they'll
do anything - as well as make it up - to get it."
- Julia Roberts, Actress

"Ah, come on, Jethro. It's two for one. We've got a few bucks left from the Crap Table and nothin' better to do. It comes with all you can eat, too. Let's go for it. It's somethin' different."

"Yeah, but, what the heck is 'A Happening,' Herb?"

Herb read the flyer. "It says here: 'Be part of the show. Make it happen.' That sounds interesting, wouldn't ya say?"

"I donno. I guess. It will pass the time until the bus leaves."

"We can tell the folks back home about it."

"Okay, okay, okay."

After Herb and Jethro purchased their tickets to the show, they were given a champagne glass, a horn, tuxedos, and a huge fork. They were ushered into a jury box on the theatre stage with several other guests. The set was like something out of a Fellini film: A cross between a court-room and a royal court, with crystal chandeliers, tapestries, sculptured busts of dignitaries, and party decorations with carnival music in the background.

Characters in bizarre costumes stood in frozen poses here and there. The King or Plaintiff, in royal attire, sat proudly in the middle of the jury box. Les Garçons or Prosecuting Attorneys, in pirate costumes, stood paused in the midst of slashes with their swords, before a large, empty dinner table. The Head Chef or Judge, in a white apron and puffy white hat, was slouched on his desk. The Bus Boy or Defense Attorney, dressed with a shirt and tie and white apron, was holding up a white wash cloth. The Court Jester or Court Clerk, holding a tattered bible in one hand with the other hand in sworn up position, wore a Jester's tasseled cap, patched jumpsuit, and a stupid grin. The Queen Mother, dressed in jeans and a man's T-shirt that read "Oedipus Ate Here," was about to place a large, white tablecloth on the large, empty dinner table. Huddled in a corner chair, sat The Defendant or Juicy Young Mother, holding The Babe, her child, in a tight embrace. Side Dishes or Witnesses were also seated: A Squash Player, in a yellow shorts outfit, holding a racket, and The Pudding wearing a brown suit and tie.

Act I

As the show opens, The King laughs and socializes with the Guests. They joke and drool over the menu. He shows them the cue cards they are to follow. The Guests and King are served champagne. They are dressed to kill and ravenous, anticipating the first bite and ready to witness some action.

Everyone rises as The Head Chef, with several shots of whisky under his belt, raises his head, pulls out a flask, sips, and glazes over the menu. He swishes the whisky around in his mouth, swallows it, and smiles. "Who, I mean, what are we cooking today? Hum, Hum. Appetizer: A Squash Player, Pudding, and the Main Course: Juicy Young Mother. Ha! Sounds delectable," he mumbles and grins, and points to a framed degree behind him. And then his head droops forward. The degree says Gastronomic Science from the College of UC Nothing.

Les Garçons, with sharp swords and tongues, approach the Bench. They slash to the left and they slash to the right, in unison. The King shows Cue Card 1 to the Guests: The Guests clap with admiration and shout, "It's a gala!"

Bowing to the audience, Les Garçons turn sharply towards The Head Chef, poking him awake, and whispering in his ear, "Remember, it's one jab for 'Sustained' and two jabs for 'Overruled'."

Startled back to consciousness, The Head Chef giggles and nods his head. "Yes, yes, of course." Now, he knows what he is to concoct as the "yes" man for the prosecution.

Les Garçons announce, "Welcome one and all, to the Royal Feast, sponsored by the King of the Court." The King takes a bow, showing the next cue card. The Subjects clap. "We are here today to try a Juicy Young Mother. Is she fit to be packaged with The Babe? We shall prove that she is not!"

The Queen Mother slaps the white table cloth on the Big Dinner Table. Prodded, the Guests clap and blow their horns. The Queen Mother strikes a match that lights a fire pit near the Juicy Young Mother's Chair.

Les Garçons announce, "To whet your appetite for the Main Course, we now serve you the Appetizer, A Squash Player. The Guests slide to the edge of their seats. A Squash Player takes the stand and raises his right hand for The Court Jester.

"Do you swear to tell a pack of lies, the whole pack of lies, and nothing but the pack of lies, so help you God?" asks The Court Jester.

"I am a Straight Shooter. I do," answers A Squash Player.

"Objection! We are looking for the truth here, nothing but the truth," interjects The Bus Boy.

Les Garcons jab The Head Chef twice. "Overruled," says The Head Chef.

"Now, A Squash Player, it says here that you have a graduate degree from UCBS in Mind Bending. Is that correct?"

"UCBS is my good old Alma Mater."

"Is it a lie that you carefully analyzed the Main Dish, based on seeing and talking with her in person?"

"You bet. Yes, that is a lie."

"Good going. Now, tell the Court what you've concluded."

"Separate packaging for The Juicy Young Mother and The Babe. Definitely separate packaging. The Juicy Young Mother has not been properly cured to be in the same container with The Babe. She's an unfit dish, very bitter. If put in the same container, she will taint The Babe. Comes from bad stock, unfit for consumption."

On cue, the Guests swallow the Squash: "Oh-h-h, harm The Babe… Unfit, unfit, unfit, bitter, bitter, bitter. BAD STOCK!"

"Objection!" shouts the Bus Boy. Les Garcons give the Head Chef two more pokes.

"Overruled," says the Judge, as his head sinks back onto the bench.

Les Garçons take their swords and examine the sharp edges. On cue, the Guests stomp their feet and stab the air with their large forks as they cheer, "Sever. Sever. Sever."

A Squash Player starts to leave the stand. The Bus Boy darts up. "I'm not done with the Appetizer!"

"You call yourself a Straight Shooter, and you swear to be a liar. That doesn't make sense."

"But it works. Power Players play to win."

"But you never even saw her before today. How can you pass judgment on her?"

"UCSB and years of Mind Bending experience are the keys to my success."

"Hum! Thank you. That will be all for now."

"No problem."

"I'd like to call to the stand The Pudding, someone who actually knows the Juicy Young Mother."

The Pudding takes the stand and raises his right hand for The Court Jester. "Do you swear to tell a pack of lies, the whole pack of lies, and nothing but a pack of lies, so help you God?"

"I swear to tell only the truth."

"The truth?" Remark the Jester, the Guests, and the King, in unison.

"Is it true that as her Psychoanalyst, you have counseled the Juicy Young Mother for five years?" The Bus Boy asks.

"Yes. It has been my pleasure to treat and to know her."

The King confers on the side lines with Les Garçons.

"What did you counsel her for?" The Bus Boy resumes.

"She suffered from improper labeling. She didn't know who she was."

"And do you feel that your counseling has helped her?"

"Yes, most definitely. She is cured. She is confident and assertive now."

"In your professional opinion, is she fit to be packaged with her child?"

"Unquestionably. She is a capable and loving mother."

"No further questions, Your Honor."

The Head Chef snores. Les Garçons wake him and prop him up.

Les Garçons question The Pudding. "Pudding, huh? You stated that you not only treated the patient, but that it was a pleasure to know her. Just tell the Court, how well did you know her? Did you find her attractive? Did you try to hug and kiss her? Isn't it true that you were a little sweet on her?"

"Whatever I felt for her personally had no effect on my treatment of her. I am a married man."

"Thank you, Pudding. That will be all."

"But...."

"You may step down now." On cue, the Guests spit out the pudding.

The King smirks and nods to Les Garçons to bring forth the tantalizing meat. Les Garçons place their long blades in their sheaths, and set a large cutting board on the center of the table. The Guests again slide to the edge of their seats, ready for the carving. The King and The Subjects stab their forks in the air, and shout: "Sever, sever, SEVER!"

The Bus Boy sneaks up close to The Head Chef and gives him a poke. "There is no reason, no grounds to separate them. I propose that the Court appoint Fair Player to examine the King and the Juicy Young Mother."

"Sustained," says The Head Chef.

Intermission: The Guests are treated to a mad-cap light show that is beamed throughout the room with deafening loud music. It lasts about 10 minutes.

Act II

It is a week later: Fair Player is sworn in.

"Do you swear to tell only lies?" asks the Court Jester.

"I am about fairness. I am here to tell the truth, of course."

"So, what is your version of the truth?" ask Les Garçons.

"I have examined both of them. The father, the self-appointed King, is a classic narcissist and a sociopath. It would be harmful for the child to be raised by him. He charms, lies, cheats, and threatens to get what he wants. The mother is a loving mother and fit to raise her child."

Boldly, The Bus Boy says, "There you have it, folks. The Court-Appointed Fair Player recommends that the child stay with the mother."

Les Garçons are closer to the bench than The Bus Boy, and quickly poke The Head Chef twice.

"Overruled!" utters The Head Chef.

Chaos ensues in the court. Les Garcons grab the recorded testimonies from the Court Jester and toss them in the fire pit. Flames leap up in the pit. Les Garçons whisper something in the Head Chef's ear. He responds with a rehearsed message: "All testimony in this case related to The Juicy Young Mother has been redacted. The father is obviously a mature adult with substantial assets. He is The King, after all. It would be in the best interest of the child to reside with him. And The Juicy Mother will be denied all access to The Babe."

"Hear, Hear! Yay!" shout the cued Guests. The King gloats. The Juicy Young Mother is horrified, holding on tight to The Babe. The Queen Mother laughs. Les Garçons, with the help of The Court Jester, drag and push the Juicy Young Mother and Babe down on the cutting board.

"NO! What are you doing? You can't take my baby. You can't separate us."

"Let go, woman! Let go! Let go now! TENDERIZE." Les Garcons shake the Juicy Young Mother up and down. They swing her back and forth, until she goes limp like a rag doll.

Through it all, the Babe dangles from her side. The Juicy Young Mother howls as they hold her still with a 2-pronged pitch fork.

The Guests are energized. "SEVER. SEVER. SEVER! This is some show! Wow! We wouldn't have missed this for the world."

Les Garcons draw out their swords and with one chop, slice The Juicy Young Mother and Babe apart. Blood from the Juicy Young Mother spurts on the floor. She is left on the cutting board.

"Nice job, Garçons. You've earned your tip," snickers The King.

A Bus Boy wraps the injured Juicy Young Mother's arm in the wash cloth, and drops another one onto the blood on the floor. He then picks it up and waves it in front of the bleary-eyed Head Chef.

"OBJECTION!" He dashes to get closer to The Head Chef, but Les Garçons get there first and poke him twice.

"Overruled!" states The Head Chef. A food timer goes off on his desk, and he is wide awake. This ends the Feast. "Thank you all for coming."

Les Garçons toss The Babe over the fire to The Queen Mother. The Babe cries as the flames scorch her leg. The Queen Mother catches the seared child in a bread basket and rocks the basket back and forth as The Babe wails.

The King pats The Guests on their heads with a scepter, as they leave the Show Room, bowing and chanting: "In the best interests of the child. In the best interests of the child. In the best interests of the child." They are glad to have tried the Juicy Young Mother and to have given her her just desserts.

Jethro and Herb return their costumes and props. They are elated after the show. Now, they had something interesting to tell their wives that would make the women overlook all the money their husbands had lost in Vegas. They caught the bus and thanked their lucky stars that they were only Guests in the Dinner Show.

A Glimpse

"Men are not prisoners of fate, but only prisoners of their own minds."
~ Franklin D. Roosevelt, President

Glenda marveled at the expressive skills of the actors and dancers who performed "The Mandala Improvisation" in her dance workshop at Maui Community College. *They are like magnificent flowers opening to the sun, and around them are shimmering light particles suspended in the air.*

She joined her students that evening at an upcountry party where she met the gaze of Baba Ram Dass, a leader of new age thinking. His face radiated as he smiled at her. He looked at her like he had always known her. *To be in his presence is a joy. His book **Be Here Now; Now Be Here** is my bible. What a perfect day!* She took a rest on the couch and closed her eyes. She saw herself in the middle of a still pond with concentric circles radiating from her body. *I am totally here now. Oh, a blank screen. I am fulfilled and relaxed and ready for what will appear next in my life.* When she opened her eyes, a tall, blond handsome man with a warm smile and a lithe but strong body was studying her face.

"Good morning, lovely lady."

"Ha, is it morning already?"

"It is if you want it to be. You just woke up, didn't you?"

"Oh, come on."

Regarding her statement as an invitation, he sat down next to her. Startled, she immediately sat up.

Who is this Prince Charming? Who is this attractive, clever guy? "Where did **you** come from?"

"Nowhere in particular, but I know where I am going."

"You do? Okay, where are you going?"

"Nevada City, California, to study with a Master Carpenter."

"Nevada City? Are you serious?" *He is going to the place where my daughter was born and lives with her father! Oh, my God.*

"Quite. Want to come with me?"

"What? I think we just met. Are you serious?" *This is uncanny.*

"You already asked me that. I am quite serious. Okay?"

"Okay, okay, I know, I know. But, I don't even know you."

"Start knowing me, now. I don't leave for a week."

"In a week? Are you crazy?"

"Maybe, don't know unless you try."

"Try?"

"Try me."

"Oh! I see."

He just smiled at her, not saying a word.

"Okay, okay. I will need to cancel some of my classes in Honolulu." *I must be nuts! What am I saying?* "I guess we can start by telling me your name."

"Andy Brill. And yours?"

"Glenda Stuart, but I may change it."

"Change your name? Why?"

"I'll tell you later."

Glenda was about to be "the fool that rushed in." Or maybe that was "being with the fool who rushed in." *This guy is really off the wall, but so cute.* She just kept thinking about the weird twist of fate, that he was going to the place where her daughter lived. Fate was known to be fickle.

Glenda spent the next several days with Andy, before he left for the Mainland. The situation was bizarre; she couldn't make sense of it. It was like there was a force drawing her to him—and of course to where he was going, to where her child was. He, himself, was charming … but, also very strange. He had an impulsive habit of waving his arms in the air to ward off evil spirits when they made love. *Is this worth it, to see my daughter? What would Ralph, my ex, do if I showed up there? Am I destined to see her?*

Glenda had recently formed a dance company in Honolulu and had a performance coming up, and she wasn't sure if she wanted to go to Nevada City to be with him, or at all. Her dance career had just taken off in Hawaii. What lay ahead in Nevada City? There was too much uncertainty.

So, she didn't go at first. But, once he was gone, he called and sent letters every day, begging. "I'm waiting for you. When are you coming?"

"I don't know. I've got things going on here."

"Oh, come on. I know you want to be here. I want you by my side, Lady. We are good together. You can teach dance here."

It does seem like more than a coincidence that he is in the same place as my daughter. Perhaps I'll go. Maybe it is meant to be. Maybe I am being led to my daughter.

Lily, her child, was now 14 years old. She hadn't even seen a picture of her for 10 years. The Court had taken away her custody and visitation rights, and Ralph wouldn't even send pictures of her growing up as Glenda had requested. *How will I recognize her? My yoga teacher told me that my time with her was over. What if Ralph finds out I am there? Will he have me locked up? It is legally against the law for me to see my own child. Damn! That's not right! It has never been right. What do I have to lose? It's worth a shot.* So, she gave up her blooming career as a dancer in Hawaii, and hopped on a plane back to California. Things never went right for her on the Mainland; deep inside she knew that.

* * *

Glenda was hired to teach dance and yoga through adult education at the local high school and a private dance school in Grass Valley and Nevada City. She called herself Lasya; the name meant the dance of beauty, happiness, and grace in Hindu Mythology. She hoped having a different name would conceal her identity in this small town.

"Get away. Get away," Andy commanded to the "evil spirits" that he imagined encircling their love nest. There seemed to be more of them this time, all there to haunt Andy and put a damper on their relationship. Glenda was also irritated when he commanded her attention; he expected her to be at his beck and call. "You are my mate! Why aren't you helping me? You can do that stuff later." He expected her to be his sidekick in carpentry. He resented the time that she spend creating and teaching movement classes. He continued to madly wave away dozens of demons in the bedroom. "You brought them here," he said accusingly. To top it off, he stated, "I don't know if I really love you." He would burst into her creative space when she was writing or preparing classes, demanding that she do what he wanted right then. "Jump in the truck. I need your help today."

"I am giving a class tonight. I have to prepare for it."

"Don't know why I waste my time with you! You are impossible … like taming a wild horse."

That wasn't the worst of it. One afternoon, with a creepy smile on his face, he tried to push her down a hill. As a trained dancer, she was able to regain her balance and not fall.

"Why did you do that?" she questioned him.

"What?"

"Push me."

"I didn't push you. I was just playing … like kids do."

Then he gracefully lifted her into a tree, as if he were a ballet partner. There was that bizarre smile again … before, he bent her back sharply, snapping and displacing her vertebrae. After that, she had to withdraw from a new ballet company before the first performance. On another occasion, he pushed her to the ground, sat on her, and obstructed her breath with his forearm. Finally, she decided to put an end to the relationship. His violence had become life-threatening.

Fortunately, it wasn't long before she was blessed with a mellow boyfriend. Barry, her new guy, created collages from magazine clippings.

His artwork of unique juxtapositions was designed to reshape people's perceptions of reality. He was a visionary.

Barry, too, had been separated from his daughter for a long time. Recently, she came back come into his life.

One day, Barry said, "You are going to see your daughter soon."

"How do you know this?"

"I just know. You are going to see your daughter in the next couple of days."

Entranced, she laid down on her bed. *I am being carried along on a smoothly flowing river. I sense that what he says is true. He sees beyond appearances. At last, I am going to see my daughter again. This is the day I have waited for. My precious girl.*

Glenda fell asleep, and dreamt that she was in prison. *The warden said, "You can see your daughter now."*

"I can?"

A girl appeared. She didn't look like her daughter. This girl had red hair and freckles; Lily had a dark complexion and dark brown hair. But what she appeared like didn't matter; she knew that the girl was Lily. They were enveloped in a body of sparkling light particles. "Lily, my dearest, I am so happy to see you." Lily smiled and walked away. "Wait, wait, Lily. I want to talk to you. I want to hug you. I want...." As the girl walked away, Glenda noticed her buoyant and even rhythm. Glenda wouldn't forget Lily's walk. When she awakened, she was ready to see her in real life.

Every Friday, before picking up her paycheck at the high school, Glenda fasted on juice and vegetable broth from fruits and vegetables that she picked from her garden. When fasting, she felt weightless. On paycheck day, she always scanned the girls in the hallway at the high school, hoping to recognize her daughter.

The day arrived. The hallway was empty. It was the last day of school before summer vacation. Most of the students were gone. Someone walked out of the Girl's bathroom behind her, and she heard and felt the rhythm from the dream. They were walking in unison in the same buoyant and even pace; that is how she knew it was her. She glanced back. *She is built like me … a short-waist and long legs. It's her; it's my daughter.*

When they reached the front door, she opened it for her. "What's your name?" Glenda asked, already knowing the answer.

"Lily."

"Lily Stuart?"

"Yes. Who are *you?*"

Here is my opportunity. A chance in a lifetime. "I am Glenda Stuart, your mother."

Lily spun around in a circle before sinking down onto the step at the school entrance. With her chin resting on her hand, she looked up at Glenda, her mother, and said, "I should have known." When Lily smiled, Glenda felt a stream of love flow into her heart. "I've seen pictures of you."

They hugged. "Oh, it is so wonderful to see you, Sweetheart." Tears rolled down Glenda's cheeks.

"What are you doing here?" Lily said, dispassionately.

"I just picked up my paycheck. I teach adult movement classes for the high school. I also teach at Marianne's Dance School. Maybe you can come sometime."

"I've taken drill team classes from Marianne."

"Do you like to dance?"

"Oh, yes. I love to dance. Oh, here comes my Mom. Uh … I mean my Step Mom."

"Oh!" Glenda watched as a blonde woman drove up. She had a scowl on her face when she saw Glenda. It was the blonde beautician, the one that had lived down the street when Glenda lived there.

And then Lily was gone. Her radiant daughter had been whisked away again.

"I knew Lily in kindergarten," someone spoke. In a daze, Glenda turned to look at the girl that had been standing there, watching the reunion. She seemed to have appeared out of thin air.

"You did?"

"Lily was sent to a private school. She just came back this semester to this high school. She's been gone all this time."

"Incredible!"

"I am separated from my Mother, too."

"Oh, I am so sorry to hear that."

"Yes, it is awful. She went away. I wish that I could see her again."

Glenda hugged her. "Miracles can happen. You just saw one."

"I guess it could happen."

"What is your name?"

"Noreen."

The girl looked down and cried.

Glenda hugged her again and let her sob.

"Thank you," Noreen said smiling.

"Noreen, would you give this flyer of my classes to Lily, so she will know where to call me?"

"I will," she promised. "I have to go now. My Dad will wonder where I am."

"Goodbye, Noreen." Glenda watched the girl walk away.

* * *

A couple of days later, Glenda's phone rang. It was Ralph, her ex. "Were you spying on Lily at school?"

Can you believe that? Spying on my own child? What nerve!

"No, of course not."

Ralph continued a fueled interrogation. "What are you doing here? Why did you come here?"

"I was invited by a guy I met in Hawaii. He was moving here and wanted me to come with him."

The flood of questions continued.

"Is that right? Are you engaged or something?"

"No, we are no longer together."

"So then, why are you still here?"

"I am teaching dance and yoga here. And of course, I'd hoped to see Lily."

"You shouldn't have upset her. You've disturbed her, you know. You've confused her. She considers Anita her mother now. She doesn't need you in her life."

She doesn't need her mother? You asshole!

"I want to see her again."

"I don't know if that's possible, at this point."

"Why not?"

"I'll think about it. Come to my office and we will discuss it."

"Okay, when?"

"Tomorrow at 2."

"Okay. I'll be there at 2."

Glenda hung up the phone, stunned by the conversation, and fearful about seeing him again. *Why do I have to beg to see my own child? I don't want to ever see him again, the son-of-a-bitch! But, it is the only way to get to my daughter. I have to do it.*

"Well, hi. It's been a long time," Ralph said with a stuck smile, when she arrived. She remembered that phony grin. Before realizing it, she was engulfed in a hug, an unwanted, unsolicited iron grip. She pulled away. He pulled her closer. "You know, Glenda, I have always loved you." Then, as he was about to kiss her, she extricated herself.

"Call me Lasya. I am no longer Glenda. I am Lasya now!"

He was speechless.

"When can I see Lily?"

"Okay, okay. Miss Las—, Las what?"

"Lasya."

"Sure, okay. How about after school tomorrow, at the house?"

"Fine. I'll be there." *Damn Bastard!*

* * *

52

At 2:30 the next afternoon, Glenda sat in her parked jalopy in their driveway, after ringing the front doorbell, and being told by Anita, Ralph's new wife, that Lily was not there and she didn't know when she would return. "May I see her room?"

"No, that is not possible," she curtly stated, and shut the door.

It was December ... freezing. snow blanketed the ground. The rattling heater in Glenda's old heap barely worked. Glenda held onto her big dog to keep warm. She shivered as she waited for Lily to return. *He said I could see her. Why aren't they here?*

There was a small house on the other side of the driveway. She drove her car into to some bushes to camouflage it and knocked on the door.

Her former mother-in-law answered the door ... holding a shotgun. "Whoa!"

"I don't mean any harm, Mazy. You've always been like a mother to me. Please let me come in to wait for Lily. It's freezing outside." It worked. Mazy put the gun down and allowed her to sit with her in her living room.

The old woman babbled nervously, something about her doctor son's pending lawsuit.

"What's that? He's being sued, you say?"

"Yes. I don't know what I did wrong. I raised him good."

"Why is he being sued?"

"I planned a good life for us. I don't know what I done wrong." She continued to talk incoherently and didn't seem to hear Glenda's questions.

Glenda heard the sound of a motor; a car was coming up the driveway. She arose and scrambled out of the house to greet her daughter. Excitedly, Lily flew into her arms. She breathed deeply, inhaling the sweet fragrance of her child.

"Come in! I want you to see my room."

They were visiting only a short while, when Ralph and Anita called Lily into the living room. Glenda couldn't make out their conversation from the other room, but she sensed trouble. When Lily returned, she was real excited. "Guess what? I'm going to Europe next semester to study! You can't be part of my life now."

And that was it, just like that. It was as if a huge wave had tugged on Lily and pulled her out to sea, and then barreled back to shore to smack Glenda in the side, leaving her buried in the sand. Just like that! *How foolish to have expected anything more. I had no choice. The current that separated us was too strong.* Shattered, she left the house, cancelled her classes, and returned to Hawaii to heal.

That's just how fickle fate can be.

Opportunity/Crisis Knocks

危機
危机

~ Chinese character for a point where things change

One night, while lounging in her bathtub, Angela feels something glide along her arm. It feels slippery like a snake. She shifts quickly to her side and stares down at the bathwater. It is only a strand of her long brown hair floating by. As she pulls the stopper out of the tub, she watches the hair slide down the drain. She gets out of tub, dries off, wraps herself in a robe, and goes into the main room. Exhausted, she disrobes, pulls down the Murphy bed, crawls in, and falls asleep. About an hour later, she starts up when she hears someone shout her name. She looks around, but no one is there. BUT, she then hears and feels a sharp whack at the base of her skull. *OUCH!* She looks at a pillow at the edge of her bed; it's glowing in the dark. Distressed and confused, she gets up and throws on some clothes, boots, and a jacket.

Knowing that the San Francisco Hospital is just up the hill, she leaves her apartment and heads in that direction. At the top of a slope, she sees lights glowing and an emergency room sign.

The sidewalk appears to waver. She almost loses her balance several times, but manages to keep herself steady by focusing on the cracks.

The Receptionist in the emergency room sees her and hands her a form. In a matter of fact voice, she says, "Bring it back to me when you are done."

Angela takes the form and sits down. After a moment, she shakes her head and mumbles, "My name, my name. What is my name? How could I forget my name?" She returns to the reception desk, and gives back the form.

The Receptionist glances at the form. "It's empty."

"I can't fill it out. I forgot everything."

"Right. Hum. Have a seat. Someone will be with you shortly."

After about an hour, Angela is tapped and told to follow a lady down a hallway to an office. Angela sits down opposite a woman in grey, who is locked into her computer. The woman fires a series of questions at her.

"Why are you here?"

"Strange things are happening to me."

The Woman in Grey clicks on the "Delusions" box on her screen. "What drugs are you on?"

"Only a little marijuana, now and then."

The Woman in Grey clicks on the "Marijuana" box on her screen. "Are you suicidal?"

"No. It's nothing like that."

The Woman in Grey clicks on the "Non-Suicidal" box on her screen. "Why are you here?"

"I answered that question. I told you. Strange things ... snakes, glowing pillows, wavering pavement ... voices ...."

"What drugs are you on?"

Angela stands up. "You are just a robot, aren't you?"

"Are you suicidal?"

Angela backs up to the door and opens it.

"Thank you for visiting the San Francisco Hospital Emergency Room. Please pick up an evaluation form on your way out."

Angela exits the room and leaves the hospital. Her head has cleared up and she walks quickly back to her apartment.

The next day is a dreary one. Looking out the window at the rain pelting down on the fire escape, she thinks about how bored and unhappy she is with her life. *Maybe the jolt I had last night was a sign.* Janis Joplin sings on the radio about when you don't have anything else, you have freedom.

"*Janis, you right. I 'ain't got nothing left to lose. No family. Hate my job. It's always cold and damp here. Nothin'. I gotta leave, go somewhere warm and sunny. I know, Hawaii! I'll go and just lie on the beach, listen to the ocean, watch the palm trees sway. Ah, perfect. I'm going. May as well be free.*"

Dancing in the Void

*"I have discovered that it is necessary, absolutely necessary, to believe
in nothing. That is, we have to believe in something which has no
form and no color – something which exists before all forms and colors
appear. This is a very important point. No matter what god or doctrine
you believe in, if you become attached to it, your belief will be based
more or less on a self-centered idea... In constantly seeking to actualize
your ideal, you will have no time for composure. But if you are always
prepared for accepting everything we see as something appearing from
nothing... then at that moment you will have perfect composure."*
~ Zen Mind, Beginner's Mind, by D.T. Suzuki.

One morning, in the Wailuku Laundromat, Laura, a petite young
woman, with hair tangled and bleached by the sun, mumbles to herself,
"What a life. Running, always running away. I'm tired of it." She coughs
as she yanks clothes out of her stained backpack and tosses them into
the washing machine.

"Running away? From what?" asks a strong, neatly-attired young
woman at one of the folding tables.

"What?" Startled, Laura looks up. "Was I talking out loud?" She
turns to face the woman.

"Well, not exactly. But I did hear something about 'running away'."

"Yep, that's how it's been," Laura says, shaking her head and
coughing more.

"Looks like you haven't washed clothes for a while, either."

"True, true. That is true," Laura replies, as she fills the washer with the rest of her clothes. She fishes around for some quarters in the pocket of her back pack, and places them in the slots on the machine.

"May I ask why you are running away? Maybe I can help."

"No place to stop, no home. It is impossible to find a decent place to live on Maui. Every place turns into another party. Non-stop! I need a place to rest, to settle down."

"That is quite true these days, with the wave of people coming here in search of Paradise."

"Paradise … right, ha! I guess I'm part of that wave. It came down with a crash. It's a cosmic joke … one party after another … everybody stoned all the time. I just want to live peacefully on this beautiful island." Laura cries and coughs. "And, I'm sick too."

"That is obvious. Have a drink of water?" The woman holds out a filled glass to her.

In a break from coughing, Laura manages to utter, "Thanks." Exhausted and disgusted, she drops onto an old metal chair. Nodding her head, she says, "Yeah, I've probably got pneumonia, too, from smoking so much dope and being on the road. What a mess my life is."

"I'm sorry that things haven't worked out the way you expected. Sounds like you're ready for a change."

"Oh, that's for sure." Laura starts to laugh, but out comes a series of coughs.

"On the road? From where?"

"Kaupo."

"Paniolo country. Not a place for a Haole girl."

"Oh, so I discovered. I barely got out alive."

"Really? What happened?"

"A German Paniolo took a fancy to me and was coming to claim me. But I escaped with my backpack the night before."

"A good thing you did. Where are you staying now?"

"In the hotel down the street, the one over the bar. It's noisy."

"Oh, that place. Yes, raucous! What's next? Where you headed?"

"I'm gonna go to Honolulu. Hopefully, get a job, find an apartment. I'm totally disillusioned."

"Totally?" The woman laughs. She is delighted to hear this. Laura looks at her warily.

"Yes, TOTALLY!"

"Good. Time to visit the Zendo."

"What? Where? What are you talking about? This is not a laughing matter."

"Oh, no. I am not laughing at you, but happy for you that you have reached a threshold."

"A threshold? Is that what this is called? That is funny. Explanation, please."

"After disillusionment, comes Zen."

"Hum, really?"

"It's a matter of timing."

"Timing? What do you mean 'timing'?"

"Meeting me at this point, when you are totally disillusioned, to let you know that there is another way to see things."

"Like what?"

"Like AS THEY ARE."

"Ah, ha, ha. The way things are … is dreadful."

"Depends on your perspective. Zen practice can change how you see things."

"Zen can do that?"

"Yes."

"Whoa! What do you mean? How? How can anything ever change all I've been through? My whole life has been a catastrophe."

"It can't change the past, just how you see it. It's a personal experience, a practice. Come to the Zendo and find out for yourself. Before you go back to Honolulu, why don't you pay a visit?"

"They allow visitors there?"

"Yes. Come by for the weekend. You can stay overnight and have vegetarian meals for only $7."

"Only $7? Sounds great! What's your name?"

"Jill. And yours?"

"I have been going by Maya. It's my stage name. I am a dancer."

"Maya? 'Maya' is a dangerous handle."

"What do you mean, dangerous?"

"Maya means illusion. And you said you are now disillusioned."

"Yeah. I guess that name doesn't fit anymore."

"It's probably time to use your real name and dispel appearances."

"Appearances, illusions, same thing?"

"Yes, they are."

"Wow! This is starting to sound interesting. I admit I've always hoped that I would find a deeper meaning for what life has handed me. I am Laura. That's who I really am."

"Good to meet you, Laura."

"Cool. Where is this Zendo?"

"It's in a beautiful place, in Haiku, upcountry. I'll draw you a map. Do you have a car?"

"No, just my feet."

"Um, I figured so. Okay. Then you'll have to hitch. It's 30 miles away."

"I can do that when I have to. I just hope that I don't meet any more crackpots on Speed. My last hitch, down the mountain from Kula, almost cost me my life."

"If they have glassy eyes and look high, don't accept the ride. Look for a single lady on her way home from work. That is safer."

"You talk a lot about being safe."

"You're feeling sorry right now, aren't you? You have been quite vulnerable, right?"

"That's true.'

"It takes effort, or should I say intention, to be safe. You have a choice."

"Intention … choice. You have me thinking in a whole new direction, Jill."

"The safe direction."

"Safe sounds good."

"Here's the map. Request a ride to Four Corners in Haiku. When you get there, take a walk for about a quarter of a mile on the dirt road to your left, going east. It will take you to the Zendo. You will see a gate with the OM sign at the top. Okay?"

"Okay. Thanks, Jill."

"You're welcome. I will tell them that you are coming. Ask for the Roshi, or his wife, Marie."

"The Roshi?"

"That is what the Zen Master is called. See you tomorrow. Get a good night's rest. Take care of yourself." Jill brings her palms together and bows from the waist towards Laura. "Gassho."

Laura also bows and repeats the new mysterious word, "Gassho."

* * *

As they travel, the road up to Haiku inclines gradually to 800 feet above sea level. The secretary on her way home to Haiku lets Laura off at Four Corners. Laura thanks the driver and walks to the beginning of the dirt road. For a few moments, she is immobile, awed by the fragrance of the tall Eucalyptus trees and their clusters of long sharp leaves, rustling in the gentle wind. The air is fresh. As she walks on the rugged dirt road, she runs her palm lightly along the soft ferns and small purple Thai orchids that grow out of the raw, red dirt embankments. She feels connected to the earth and in heaven at the same time. In a clearing, she spots the ocean that appears motionless in the distance, like a beautiful painting. *Am I in Paradise, at last?*

She arrives at a modest wood dwelling, offset from the road. On the arched gateway trellis is the OM sign that Jill had mentioned. She knows, as a student of Yoga, that OM means all nature in harmony. *I feel like I am coming home.*

Facing the house, she sees a well-maintained vegetable garden and fruit trees on the left, and a green lawn on the right with tiger lilies gracing the pathway to the house, like a picture out of *Better Homes and Gardens*. Already, even before entering the Zendo, she feels her perception changing.

Stillness pervades the silence, as Laura observes the Zen students filing into a meditation hall off of the porch. They are all dressed in black: black robes, black pants, black shirts, and black jackets. Laura smiles, but no one looks up or smiles back. They are very serious. She watches each one bow with palms together upon entering the hall, the same gesture that Jill had made at the Laundromat. Through the screened windows, she sees them bow again, and then sit down on black cushions and face the wall. A young man sees her and meets her on the porch. Softly he asks, "May I help you?"

"I am here to see the Roshi."

"Please have a seat. I will get him."

Laura plops down, removing her heavy backpack. She muffles her cough, so as not to disturb those meditating. A tall, gaunt man with a goatee greats her with a bow and palms together. The student bows the same way, and returns to meditate in the hall.

"You are Laura, correct?"

"Yes. Jill sent me."

"Very good. I am the Roshi. Welcome. Come this way."

She stands up and picks up her pack. He quietly escorts her to a bedroom.

"Please make yourself at home in this room."

Coughing, Laura smiles and sets down her pack in the bedroom.

Taking note of her cough, he says, "My wife Marie is visiting down the hall with her brother, a doctor. He will be in to see you soon." Laura smiles. They bow and he leaves. Laura stretches out on a foam sleeping mat on the floor and falls asleep. Later, when she awakens, she gazes out the window at lush green plants and is soothed by colorful birds twittering and flitting through the palm fronds. The doctor appears and gives her medicine. The Roshi and Marie look on with love and concern. Soothed, Laura falls into another peaceful sleep.

After several days of rest, Laura meets with the Roshi, the Zen Teacher, in his office. He looks at her seriously, with a slight smile.

"Laura, how are you feeling today?"

"Much better, thank you." Coughing, she adds, "I guess it will take a little time to feel all better. I've had pneumonia before."

"Of course. And we will help you all we can."

"I am very grateful for that."

"I trust that in coming here, you are in earnest in wanting to start a Zen practice. Is that so?"

"It is, very much so."

"I'm happy to hear that. Why do you want to meditate?"

"I want to make sense of my life. It's been so strange ... so painful."

"I understand. You are not alone in this. It is a pleasure to meet you, Laura, and to have you join our Sangha."

"Thank you. What is a Sangha?"

"The Sangha is your community here at the Zen Center."

"Community, Roshi? That's not something that I am used to. I am pretty much a loner. I've been hurt a lot in the past."

"Focusing on your breathing will keep you in the present. The past is illusive."

"How do I do that?"

"Like this." The Roshi, pulling his chair back from his desk, lowers his eyelids and sits up very straight. He places his left palm in his right with his thumbs touching, resting his arms in his lap, rocks his upper body slightly from side-to-side and begins to breathe audibly and speak softly. "Inhale one, Exhale two, Inhale three, Exhale four ... please join me, Laura."

Laura mirrors what the Roshi has shown her and begins counting her breaths.

"Now, count your breaths silently from one to ten, and then start again at one."

For a few moments, they sit quietly in meditation, counting breaths. When Roshi taps the desk twice, they both open their eyes.

The Roshi brings his palms together and bows towards Laura, saying "Gassho."

Laura does the same. "That sure did relax me. What does 'Gassho' mean?"

"It means I recognize and honor the Buddha, your awakened nature. It is a show of respect for another."

"Ah, respect. That is quite lovely and refreshing." She coughs slightly.

They Gassho once again, and Laura rises and leaves the room, feeling a sense of belonging and calmness that she has never felt before.

* * *

Once Laura's cough subsides, she begins her Zen practice with the Sangha. Inside the Dojo, the meditation hall, is an altar, at the front of the room. There sits a statue of a rotund Buddha, a stick of burning incense, a flower arrangement, and a kikosaku (a long flat stick). Following the other students, Laura bows at the door to the Buddha, walks to a zafu, (a meditation cushion) facing center, and bows to the Sangha. Turning towards the wall, she bows towards the cushion and then sits on the zafu facing the wall. As the Zendo Monitor strikes a small bell three times, the students rock back and forth to settle into their meditation. The Monitor remarks loudly, "Thoughts have no substance. Let them pass through." Laura doesn't quite understand that. She counts her breaths, as instructed by the Roshi.

When it is time for Dokusan, a formal visit with the Roshi, Laura asks, "What does it mean that 'thoughts have no substance'?"

"They come and they go."

"Where do they come from? Where do they go?"

"Nowhere."

"Nowhere? But, I need to be somewhere."

"Ah! You are not your thoughts. Your thoughts are not your true nature."

Laura appears confused, but curious. The Zen Master brings his palms together and bows to Laura. He is done speaking. She bows and leaves the room, and returns to the Zendo hoping for less thoughts and a glimpse of her true nature.

* * *

Laura, now in fully engaged in the practice, arises at dawn. She exercises silently on the porch with the other students, prior to the first sitting. After three 25-minute sitting periods, interspersed with 5 minutes of Kinhin (walking meditation), she eats breakfast with the Sangha. With the exception of Sutras (chants), they eat in silence. The silence continues as they go to work either in the garden or in the house, with a tea break, followed by more work, a formal lunch, work, and the mild conversation at dinner, more meditation, shower, and bedtime at 9. It is pretty much the same every day, with only one day off during the week. On that day off, the Sangha goes into town for a busy day of shopping and fun. By the end of the day, they are glad to get back to the peace and quiet of the Zendo.

Every morning before mediation they recite the **Great Vows for All**.

> *The many beings are numberless,*
> *I vow to save them.*
> *Greed, hatred, and ignorance rise*
> *endlessly, I vow to abandon them.*

Dharma gates are countless,
I vow to wake to them.
The Buddha's way is unsurpassed,
I vow to embody it fully.

And the **Ti-Sarana**.

I take refuge in the Buddha
I take refuge in the Dharma
I take refuge in the Sangha.

Try as she might to not be distracted by her thoughts during meditation, in order to see her true nature, Laura is easily sidetracked. When she sees and hears the Monitor slapping the shoulders of the students during Zazen (meditation) with the Kiosaku, it calls up old thoughts of her being beaten as a child. After the Roshi assures her that it doesn't hurt, but rather helps further the practice, Laura tries it and finds that it helps her keep her concentration on her breath. But there are also sutras that distract her, like one that contains the following:

"... Be especially sympathetic and affectionate with foolish people, particularly with someone who becomes a sworn enemy and persecutes us with abusive language. That very abuse conveys the Buddha's boundless loving-kindness. It is a compassionate device to liberate us entirely from the mean-spirited delusions we have built up with our wrongful conduct from the beginningless past. With our open response to such abuse we completely relinquish ourselves, and the most profound and pure faith arises. At the peak of each thought a lotus flower opens, and on each flower there is revealed a Buddha. Everywhere is the Pure Land in its beauty. We see fully the Tathagata's radiant light right where we are. May we retain this mind and extend it throughout the world so that we and all beings become mature in Buddha's wisdom."

Laura is totally frustrated by those passages, having suffered considerable abuse during her life. *Obviously, I will never "become mature in Buddha's wisdom."*

* * *

During the Tea Break, Laura asks Roshi, "How can I forget the past?"

"Remember, just this! Just this moment. That is all there is."

"But I want more. I want to know why. How can I see the deeper meaning? I don't want to suffer any more."

"Are you suffering in this moment?"

"No."

"Just this, then!" the teacher repeats with a big smile.

"Oh, okay. But I can't understand why this is called a training session. What are we training for?"

"We are practicing how to live, how to see things as they are right here, right now."

"What about fun? I must confess, I am not having any fun here."

"There will be time for fun. For now, you must practice."

"I am 30 years old already. Isn't it a bit late to learn how to live, to see things differently?"

"No, not too late. Never too late."

Monotonous! Laura thinks.

Jill hangs around after tea. "How's it going, Laura?"

"Oh, okay, I guess. Actually, I am bored."

"Of course. I can understand that. Same thing every day, day after day."

"Exactly, Jill. I am not cut out for this lifestyle."

"And the lifestyle you had before wasn't boring, was it?"

"No, I was free, did what I wanted, when I wanted to."

"Did you, now? You didn't seem very happy about your 'freedom' when I met you in the Laundromat."

"Well, that's true. But I need a bit more excitement, fun, than I have here."

"I guess you have to create some fun and excitement. Have you looked in the Free Box over there on the edge of the porch?"

"'Free Box'? What's that? What's in there?" Laura walks to the edge of the porch and opens the lid of the Free Box. "Wow! What's all this stuff in here?"

"Oh, just odds and ends that people don't want or need anymore."

"Free? Wow! Hey, I like this red and orange skirt and peasant blouse. Think I'll try them on." Laura puts on the clothes and launches into a Broadway song by Jerome Kern and a dance, "Lovely to look at; delightful to know," she sings. Jill just smiles. But Laura laughs and cuts loose with her song. She is having a great time, singing and twirling around the porch. "Razzmatazz."

After a spin in the flowing skirt, she stops short, before a scowling Zen Master. "Keep it down. You are creating a disturbance. Other people are resting. This is quiet time. You should be resting, like everybody else."

"Rest time? I was just having some R & R with the clothes from the Free Box. I love to dance. I am a dancer."

"Now is not the time to dance. Now it is time to rest."

"I'll put them back."

"You can keep the clothes, but be mindful of others. This rest time is part of the schedule, part of the practice. It takes strength to meditate. Settle down." He turns sternly and walks off.

"How do you like that, Jill? Jill? Wow, Jill is gone …. She must be … resting."

Stunned, Laura returns to her room. *All I was doing was having a little fun. Jeez, can't a person have a little fun?* She lies down on her mat and rests; she *is* a bit tired.

* * *

Laura continues the practice, half-heartedly at times, frequently distracted and disturbed by the thoughts from the past that seem determined to block her progress. One day, she just doesn't show up on her cushion. At the end of the previous sitting, she exited Kinhin (the slowly moving line) and headed for her room, where she slid into her sleeping bag, thinking to herself, *At the first opportunity, I am outta here!*

Soon, there is a tap on her window. Laura peeks out of her bag and sees the Zen Master smiling at her through the blinds. *"Why is he smiling at me?"*

"Are you okay?" he asks.

"I'm okay, just tired." *"I am outta here."*

"You are completely well now, aren't you, Laura?"

"Yes, but…," Laura starts crying.

"But what? May I come in?" He enters Laura's room.

"I can't do this anymore! My thoughts of the past are driving me crazy. I don't know about finding this 'true nature' stuff. Maybe I don't have one."

"Meditating will help you to stay in the present and let go of the pain from the past. What happened years ago is now just as an accumulation of thoughts. Please come back to the training."

"And thoughts have no substance."

"RIGHT! YES!"

Laura nods and wipes her eyes.

The Zen Master brings his palms together, stands up, and bows.

Laura does the same and goes back to the Zendo to continue meditating.

At the end of the next sitting, the monitor taps her on the shoulder and points towards the door.

"Marie would like a word with you in the bath house," he whispers.

Oh, great, a lecture.

Laura enters the bath house with hesitation. She isn't looking forward to a reprimand.

"You are completely well now, aren't you, Laura?"

"Yes, but…."

"Laura, we are here to do Zazen. We are here to practice. If you cannot keep the schedule, you must leave," she states firmly.

Wow! Just like that. She's actually telling me to leave. I can't believe this. She can just dump me, like that!

"But…."

"Laura, what is the problem?"

Does she really want to know?

"I'm bored. It's boring here."

"Do you want to go back to the 'exciting' life you had before you came here … very sick?"

"No, no. I don't want to do that. I love the quiet and natural sounds here at the Zendo. It is so peaceful here."

"Yes."

"Why would you ask me to leave? I am very hurt."

"I am only asking you to leave if you can't keep the schedule."

"It's a real trade-off, isn't it?"

"Trade-off?"

"Yeah. I have to choose between peace and boredom, and chaos and fun. It doesn't seem fair or right."

"You have a lot of thoughts about how things are. In time, you might change your point of view. You might find being peaceful fun."

"Really? Is that possible?"

"It has become so for me and many others. We look forward and cherish the time to rest and be peaceful. It is a way of life for us, as we hope that it will be for you."

"I sort of know what you mean. There are times that I actually forget to suffer here. I have suffered for so much of my life. There are times when I am so grateful for the peace that I feel inside."

"I take it that you will be keeping the schedule from now on?"

"Yes, I understand. I will keep the schedule," Laura replies.

Her meditation practice seems more serious now. She has taken the bodhisattva vows, along with the other Zen students. She has vowed to free sentient beings from cycles of death, rebirth and suffering. That is a tall order, but it sounds good. *I don't wish suffering on anyone, I am pretty sick of it myself.*

For the first time in her life, she is part of something greater than herself. Petty differences at the Zendo are easily released when there is work that needs to be done together or after meditation. She feels part of a Sangha, a spiritual community. Now, it doesn't matter if she is tired, or angry, or not in the mood to do something; she just does it. She works, eats, sits on her cushion, and sleeps; life is simple and she is never hung over.

* * *

One weekend, some of the Sangha members go on a hike through a forest on the side of Haleakala Crater. Laura looks forward to getting away from the routine for a while and enjoying the trees. It is a picturesque hike with koa, ohia lehua, eucalyptus, ash, cypress, and redwood trees that have been imported from all over the world.

The group has access to a cabin where they are spending the night. That evening in the cabin, June, one of the budding bodhisattvas, announces, "I am a massage therapist. I can give you all a lesson. Who would like to be massaged?"

"I would," Laura announces, and climbs up onto the table. The group of eight people gather around Laura's body, ready to follow June's instructions.

It is comforting, at first, to have her friends, her Zendo brothers and sisters, giving her all that attention. She relaxes as the students follow June's instructions. "Run your hand over an area and gently feel for muscle tension." That feels good to Laura, to have everyone's fingers dancing on her skin. It almost tickles. "When you find some tension, press a bit harder." The students press and press some more, harder and harder until it hurts. Laura begins to wonder if "they even see her" there or if she has just become some sort of punching bag. They seem suddenly possessed with a sense of power and cruelty. "And rub that area a bit more," says June. Laura feels victimized, but can't speak. She is in shock at what is happening. All she can do is think, *These are my friends, my housemates, my Sangha. We are all bodhisattvas, here to relieve each other's suffering. But, they are hurting me. How can that be?*

It gets worse. The massagers are out of control. Everyone laughs and has fun, except Laura. But she can't simply say, "Stop. You're hurting me." It is like her tongue is tied, she is afraid to make a sound. Relieved when it is over, and stunned, she runs outside to cry. She walks into the forest, where no one can see her cry. She no longer feels safe with the Sangha. It's all just like before she got to the Zendo … people abusing her. When they return to the Zendo, she goes to Dokusan, totally depressed. She tells Roshi what they did to her in the cabin.

He surprises her by saying, "You missed your opportunity."

"Opportunity? What do you mean?"

"To take command of the situation. To demand that they stop that kind of behavior."

"I was scared. I was humiliated. I couldn't believe that they were doing that to me. I thought I was safe with them. I thought that they were my friends. People shouldn't do that to their friends."

"People do all kinds of things, Laura. People are no different in the Zendo than they are out of the Zendo. People are people. It's best not to have expectations about the way things should be or how people should act. They are just what they are. They are all suffering from the wrongs done to them in their lives. 'Greed, hatred, and ignorance rise endlessly.' They may show it differently than you do. That doesn't make it right, but by following the practice, they may come to terms with their actions. Where does your suffering begin and where does it end?"

"I don't know, Roshi. Where?"

"Laura, go back to your cushion and sit with this. You are not a victim. Find out what that means to you."

The Roshi then bows, with palm to palm and says "Gassho."

Laura does the same.

Laura's goal now is to completely understand, "That very abuse conveys the Buddha's boundless loving-kindness." "It was a compassionate device to liberate" her from her delusions about suffering, about blaming herself and others for acting out of ignorance, greed, and hatred. It is time for compassion for the foolish actions of others and herself, that were not her fault or directed at her; just "wrongful conduct from the beginningless past" that arose out of misperceptions. "Now, at the peak of thought, a lotus flower can open, and on each flower there can be revealed a Buddha." Now, she sees what it means to "be mature in Buddha's wisdom."

Laura returns to her cushion. She is scathed by the past; but, back in the present, in the large, silent Dojo with the Sangha, the other students of life who are just here and nowhere else. Preconceptions dissipate, as she settles into her cushion, into nothingness, into her True Nature that is No Nature. She focuses on her breath and the mind road dims. She is calm with nowhere to go, nowhere to hide, and no need to run.

* * *

Laura stands in line with the Sangha, ready to enter the Zen Meditation Hall. Today is the day for Dharma Combat. She is ready; she is armed with a question to challenge the Roshi. The large densho bell is struck by the Monitor in the descending diminuendo pattern. Students enter the Zendo. Sitting down, each faces towards the center of the room, preparing to witness the array of students about to confront the Master.

The Roshi, in a long, dark robe, arrives. He bows to the Buddha and to the Sangha. The students bow in return. He carefully arranges his robe as he lowers himself to the floor, and slides onto the cushion located at the head of the room. Composed, but alert, he is ready to meet his students head-on. An additional cushion is set before him.

When no one else ventures forward, Laura rises up, and walks towards the teacher. She brings her palms together, bows, and then kneels onto the empty cushion. Facing him, she smiles and hesitates.

"What is your question, Laura?" the Zen Master asks.

Bravely, she responds, "What is the Dance in the Void?"

The Zen Master's eyes brighten. He grins, leans towards Laura, and peers intently into her eyes.

"What was your dance from there to here?"

Laura is lost for words and looks back at where she had sat to where she sits now. She shakes her head in confusion. She looks deeply into his eyes. All at once, he sits up very tall, lowers his eyelids, as if he is going to meditate. And then, his eyes open widely and he shouts, "Attention!"

Startled, Laura arches back and then sits speechless. He glares at her. After a pause, he sharply taps the floor with a small crooked staff on each of the following words: "One step at a time."

Signaling the end to their combat, he straightens up and leans forward in a bow to Laura.

The Light Fantastic

*'True ease in writing comes from art, not chance, as
those move easier who have learn'd to dance'.*
~ Alexander Pope, Poet

*"You can't go back and change the beginning, but you
can start where you are and change the ending."*
~ C. S. Lewis, Author

During the '70s, embedded in the San Francisco Industrial District, was a funky discotheque, frequented by the counterculture, called The Garden of Earthly Delights. It was an old night spot, not much to look at from the outside; but, from the inside one saw beyond appearances. A Cyclops statue sat on a high shelf above the red leather-trimmed bar observing the longhairs, families with dogs and children, and people in wheelchairs as they strutted, swayed, howled, wheeled, and otherwise jived to the loud rock band beneath a spinning strobe light.

One Friday night, Terry, a shapely dancer, took a seat at the bar, ordered a martini, and kept time with the music. A stocky guy headed towards her, reached his arm around behind her, and dropped an acid tablet in her drink, and let his arm fall on her shoulder.

Right in her face, he said, "Hi, Lady. You are one pretty chick."

"Thanks, I guess," she said, pulling back and withdrawing his arm. He lifted his glass to toast her. She picked up her glass and tapped his, took a long drink, and attempted to move him out of the way. He grabbed her arm and didn't budge. Instead, he winked at her.

"They call me Adam," he said, brushing against her thigh.

Moving her legs to the other side, she remarked, "Ha, Adam, like in this Garden?"

"Yeah, and you can be my Eve."

"No, thanks." She bobbed her head to the music, trying to look around him and retrieve her arm.

"You like to dance, Eve," Adam stated, as he dragged her onto the dance floor and swirled his hips. The strobe flashed over her breasts, and Adam stared at them and puckered his lips.

Disgusted, Terry moved back. Adam moved forward nonstop until he had her up against a wall.

A thin sinewy guy slid in between them and whispered in Terry's ear, "There is a game of two s-s-s-sides, but we're all on the same s-s-s-side." He slithered away to the bar, and wrapped his thin-tapered legs around a stool. Curious, Terry followed him.

"That's interesting, what you said. Tell me more, Snake Guy," Terry said.

"Call me S-s-slider."

"That is an interesting name. I guess that's what snakes do."

"It is-s-s what I do best. I take the path of least res-s-s-sistance."

"Where do I find that path? Seems like there are a lot of rocks wherever I go."

"There is really only one s-s-s-s-ide."

"How can that be? The two-sided game is the only one that I know."

The Acid kicked in. She turned her head and saw Adam changing into a wild beast, about to lunge at her. Slider wrapped his lanky body around her and pulled her away again. This time, they sank through the floor into total darkness. There was no music, only discordant sounds, screams, and uncontrolled laughter.

"What happened? Where are we?" asked Terry.

A sign flashed on and off saying: "THE BARDO PLANE".

"What is the Bardo Plane?"

Slider responded, "The place between Death and Rebirth."

"Am I dead?"

"In a manner of s-s-s-speaking. You fell from the lack of conscious-ness up there into a new awareness down here. I caught you as you fell."

"Well, thanks a lot. At least I knew who I was up there."

"Did you now? Who were you?"

"A dancer."

"Then why did you fall so hard?"

"I was scared. That beast was after me."

"It appears-s-s that you never learned how to fall up."

"What? That is a paradox."

"Ah, s-s-such is life. You need to fall up instead of apart to be on the path of least resistance."

"Okay. How does one accomplish that? Life is full of obstacles, setbacks, and disappointments."

"It's all in how you dance. It is necessary to master 'The Light Fantas-s-stic'."

"Hum, that sounds nice. Teach me that dance. What are the steps?"

"Oh, no particular step-s-s-s or dance. It's all about s-s-style."

"Style, as in…?"

"Taking one step at a time, and being light on your feet. But first, you must commit to letting the past fall away. Are you?"

"Maybe."

The setting became a lighted dance studio. "How did we get here?" Terry asked from the floor as Slider arose and smiled.

"S-s-see? Now you have a whole big studio in which to perform."

"I love being back in the studio. Will I find the Light Fantastic style here?"

"Naturally."

"Where?"

"Right where you stand and move, once you begin to move. Choose your steps, one at a time. Go for it. Be yourself. Let's see what you got."

"I don't think you'll want to see that, the real stuff inside me."

"That is precis-s-sly what I am waiting for."

"I am still hurting from things that have happened to me. I told you I've been through some really rough places in my life."

"BEEN? Oh, the pas-s-st again. The past is gone, yes-s-s? And your dance is always in the present, yes-s-s? Now, now, now! What's happening inside you right Now?"

"But, I don't have one."

"A dance or a present?"

"Both."

"Come on. You are a dancer. You always have a dance. The present is now, just this, here and now. S-s-s-tart moving, and s-s-see what comes out."

"Why am I even here?"

"You're here because you love to dance. You're here because you NEED to dance. Dance from your heart. That's what dancers-s-s do."

"My heart? My heart is broken."

"Then do a broken dance."

"You don't want to see that."

"That is exactly what I am waiting to s-s-see." Slider was losing his patience. "Your brokenness-s-s; let's see it. If you fall, I will help you. That is, after all, my specialty."

Terry started crying.

"Ohhhhh! Effective opening. Catches the audience's attention, s-s-sets the tone."

"Really! I don't want to be broken. And I certainly don't want other people to see how I feel."

"But, you ARE broken. You can't hide it. It is your dance right now. You've caught my interest. Let's s-s-see the rest, give me the whole thing."

Terry walked in circles, and then to the left and then to the right repeatedly, faster and faster, in a figure eight. She couldn't stop. Then she punched the air in every direction and stomped around the room. Her whole body shook, and shook, shook off years of pain.

"Nice formations, good routine, s-s-strong s-s-s-how of emotions-s-s. I like it," Slider said, clapping his hands.

Exhausted, Terry gave way, lost her balance, and fell to the floor.

"Bravo!" Slider shouted. "Great ending."

"This is the part where I can't get up."

"Yes-s-s, you can. Let's redo that fall part;" Slider helped her up. "Now, this time, as you fall, lift as you lower, fully extend your arms towards the ceiling, and s—s-slide out as you gorgeously land." Terry did as he instructed and easily rose up again. She felt light as air as she performed several spins around the room.

"Now you've got it, Terry. There is a dance to channel everything; that's what dancers know and do. The topic of your dance doesn't matter: happy, sad, angry, bored, etc. etc. doesn't matter. It's all about being light on your feet; that's how you rebound! Now, you know how to fall up. Welcome to The Light Fantastic! To a life of infinite possibilities."

About the Author

Arlene Cohen has lived a life punctuated by acute moments of disbelief that have inspired her to write humorous short stories with a twist of magical realism. Her first collection called ***Mostly True: Short Stories*** is available on Amazon. She has degrees from the University of Hawaii: a Bachelor's in American Studies and a Master's in Library Science. After Library School, with grants from the National Endowment for the Arts and Humanities, the Hawaii State Culture and the Arts, The Texas Heritage Musical Foundation, and The Regional Arts and Culture Council in Oregon, she performed as a Dancing Storyteller throughout the U.S. At the University of Hawaii she was an Academic Librarian, and Storytelling Instructor in the Speech Department. Arlene writes books for both children and adults. Her first book, ***Stories on the Move: Integrating Literature and Movement with Children from Infants to Age 14***, is a compilation of programs that she did as an Artist-in-the-Schools Dancing Storyteller, the highlight of her life for 30 years. The book is still in print and available on Amazon. 1,500 copies have been sold internationally to Teachers, Librarians, and Parents who use it to develop all aspects of their children's development, particularly literacy skills and movement agility. She just published a series called ***Literacy on the Move***, three fun picture books that integrate dance and stories to entertain children and develop their literacy skills. As they dance the words and images, they naturally understand their meaning. All the books are on Amazon in Kindle, hardback, and paperback editions: *The Dancing Chameleons: Literacy on the Move,* **Book 1** for Ages 2-6, *The Dancing Reptiles: Literacy on the Move,* **Book 2**, for Ages 4-8; and *The Dancing Dogs: Literacy on the Move,* **Book 3**, for Ages 5-10. Companion Coloring and Activity books are also available on Amazon. To find all of her books do one search "Arlene N. Cohen". Kindly leave a review at the bottom of the book's page. Thank you!

Website: amazon.com/author/arlenecohenauthor.com

Sutras were composed/interpreted by Zen Master Robert Aitken.